Steel City 5

Roxellana

A Sam Budda and Nick Savarese Novel

• • • •

William Lafferty

New Image Press, Pittsburgh PA

BOOKS BY
WILLIAM LAFFERTY

• • •

The Claysville Escapade

The Warehouse on 49th Street

The Well-Heeled Rapist

Liberty Bridge Is Falling Down

After the Dogfights

They Came for Our Guns, They Came for Our Freedom

Death by Popular Vote: Betrayal From Within

• • •

See the website at
www.williamlafferty.com

New Image Press
4433 Howley Street
Pittsburgh, PA 15224

FIRST EDITION
ISBN 978-0-9842963-5-4

Roxellana

Chapter 1

The ten year old Chevy had been sitting in a remote part of the WalMart parking lot all day. The manager saw it there when he came to work at 7:00 a.m. The same manager saw it again when his shift ended at 3:00 p.m. Someone was in the driver's seat, hunched a bit. The manager thought of going over to see if the person was all right, but then thought better of it. His wife was always meddling in other people's business and he criticized her for it. It was cold. He'd solved enough problems for one day.

The occupant of the car, Oscar Jameson, Head Teller at the Centurion Bank in Squirrel Hill, had been parked there since the wee hours of the morning before. Beer bottles littered the car. Empties almost filled the passenger foot well. Oscar sometimes peed in a bottle and sometimes peed in his pants. In any event, the car smelled of beer and urine. Oscar didn't seem to notice.

A person watching could see Oscar talking to himself, arguing, even loudly, sometimes with an imaginary antagonist, sleeping sometimes, and sometimes staring vacantly through the windscreen with tears running down his cheeks. By mid-morning, his hair was messed up wildly and he had wrapped a plaid scarf around his neck in several folds.

In the early evening, at dusk, there was an orange flash inside the car. Oscar Jameson had shot himself to death with a .32 Police Special Colt revolver. It had been his father's, or maybe it was his uncle's, he wasn't sure.

Chapter 2

"Roxellana." Her mother's voice was shrill on the phone. "Roxellana. Are you there?"

"Yes mother, what is it?" Roxellana stood in her dormitory room wrapped in a bathrobe, dripping from the shower. Her long brown hair hung in wet strands over her shoulders and wet footprints went from the shower room, down the hall and into her room. Her roommates had come to get her in the shower because her mother sounded frantic on the telephone.

"It's your father. For God's sake, it's your father." She broke down in uncontrolled sobbing. Finally, she stammered, "He's dead. He killed himself. For God's sake, Roxellana, he killed himself. In the car. At WalMart's."

"Oh... No."

Her mother was incoherent then. Roxellana was stunned and said nothing, just listening to her mother's plaintive cries.

"What will we do now? He's gone. No job. No one to pay the mortgage and the taxes. What will we do, Roxellana?" she wailed.

The woman was out of her mind with grief and shock, and the girl struggled with the disjunction between her father's death and the mortgage payment.

Finally, when her mother quieted down from sheer exhaustion of grief, she said, "Mom, Mom. Listen to me. You'll be fine. You'll be just fine. I'll come over as soon as I get dressed. You just make yourself a cup of tea and sit down. Will you do that?"

"Yes," the mother said, childlike, sobbing.

The police had found the body earlier in the day. In the parking lot. Oscar Jameson had put a gun to his head, pulled the trigger, and sprayed blood, skull and a gray matter on the back window and the seat. His mouth hung open, slack, and his head lay on his right shoulder, almost as if he were asleep. Asleep with a black-rimmed hole in his forehead.

Roxellana pulled on jeans and a sweater and ran her fingers through her long brown hair as she dried it with the blow drier, imagining her father's corpse lying awkwardly on a car seat in a parking lot. Uncertainty and fear raced through her mind as she stood in front of the mirror. She couldn't imagine what she would say to her mother.

• • •

A year prior to his death, Oscar Jameson's life took a turn for the worse. Overnight, as it were, he began to exhibit signs of serious illness. He lost his appetite, he couldn't sleep, he missed work at the bank for the first time in nineteen years, and his drinking, which had been progressing for years, become almost insistent. He seemed to drink himself into a stupor at every opportunity. When he was sober, he was listless and uninterested in anything, except that he was insistent on buying his teenage daughter, Roxellana, a car.

"What are you talking about?" his wife shouted at him. "We've been over this a hundred times and we agreed that she doesn't get a car. Are you nuts? We can't afford it. What are you thinking?"

"She needs a car," her husband said quietly.

"Yeah, and I need new clothes. But I'm not getting new clothes and she's not getting a car," she snorted.

"She's getting a car," her husband insisted.

"There's no reason for her to have a car. She's a seventeen year old kid, for God's sake. She skips school, she dates men twenty years older than she is, and she does nothing but complain about what we *don't* give her. And we can't afford it. Besides, we agreed ever since she started asking for a car that she couldn't have one. What's different now?"

"I changed my mind," her husband whispered.

"You're sick and you're going to the doctor," his wife told him. "There's something wrong with you, Oscar."

"There's nothing wrong with me."

"I've made an appointment. You're going."

"I'm fine," he said.

"It's tomorrow," she said.

"Leave me alone," he said.

The next day Pamela drove him to the doctor's office and he slunk into the examining room, shuffling like a ninety year old man. Pamela went with him. She pulled him by the arm. When the doctor came in, she told him Oscar's symptoms. Anyone could see, just by looking at him, that there was something wrong. The doctor did a thorough examination and ordered tests. Two weeks later he called and spoke to Pamela.

"There's nothing wrong with him, Pamela," the doctor said. He paused. "Physically."

"I can't believe it," she said.

"Has he been under a lot of stress lately?" the doctor said.

"Not that I know of," she answered. "The usual stuff. You know. The job. Roxellana. That kind of stress. But he's had that for years."

That's what Pamela thought, but that wasn't really accurate. There was a new stress in Oscar's life that she didn't know about. It was something to do with their daughter, Roxellana.

Roxellana had always been a complex, difficult child. More than once, Pamela wondered what she had done to deserve such a girl. The grade school years were filled with trauma at school. At home there were always problems when she played with other children. One minute she would be playing nicely and the next she would be hitting them. It got to the point that no parents would allow their children to play with her. That's when Oscar and Pamela began taking her to a psychiatrist. The diagnosis was that Roxellana was a sociopathic personality. The parents refused to accept this diagnosis. "What do they know?" they would say. "All children go through difficult phases."

Roxellana matured very quickly, faster than the other girls, and she very soon discovered her sexuality. She loved to flirt with other girls' boyfriends, and she would lead them on until they promised that they would never see their old girlfriends again. Then she dumped them. Needless to say, she was not popular among the other girls. When she wasn't stealing other girls' boyfriends, her time in high school was spent drinking with older men, cutting school, and experimenting with sex. Finally, she picked up a thirty year old bar-lizard as a steady boy friend.

Despite this troublesome behavior, Roxellana excelled academically. In high school, she was in the honors program, and she could get A's in any subject she chose. College, however, was not a real interest or priority for

Roxellana. She spent virtually all of her time and energy trying to get her parents to buy her a car and give her an allowance. They refused. They said they simply didn't have enough money. Roxellana said they shouldn't have had children if they couldn't afford them.

Oscar, Roxellana's father, had been teetering on the edge of manic-depression for years. He used alcohol to self-medicate. By the time Roxellana was in high school, Walter was drunk every night after work. Roxellana's incessant demands depressed him, made him feel inadequate, and made him question, as she put it, whether he should ever have been a parent. "Why can't you be like my friends' parents?" she would complain. "They don't scrimp for money. They don't say their kids can't have things."

Each of these exchanges left Oscar in a funk. He was inadequate. He was a bad parent. He knew he should never have had children. He knew he was a disaster as a father. And there was no way he could fix it, make it up to her.

When Oscar and Pamela first started talking about having children, Walter was reluctant because mental illness ran on his side of the family. His mother died in an institution and his only brother was a suicide. He was terrified that he might pass his family's mental problems on to his offspring. Pamela assured him it wouldn't happen and she wheedled and coaxed him into having a child. Now Walter hated his life and he hated his inadequacy. Just as he thought, he produced a mentally deficient child. She wasn't institutionalized, but she was unbalanced, hateful, full of herself and seemingly ruthless.

Hostilities seemed to relax a bit in Roxellana's senior year of high school when she enrolled in a film class. She learned how to use video cameras. In fact, it was all she talked about. Oscar and Pamela breathed easier: she had finally found something that interested her besides sex, money and drugs. And they were right. Film did interest Roxellana, and by the end of the semester, Roxellana used her new skill as a cinematographer to change the lives of her parents forever.

One evening when her mother was in bed and her father was drunk asleep in his chair, Roxellana set up her video camera. She pulled him out of the chair onto the floor, undressed him, stimulated him sexually, and filmed him having sex with her.

A week later, her courage puffed up by her desire for money, Roxellana presented her father with the video and told him to watch it in private. After he watched it, she said, they would talk about what kind of car he was going to buy her. He was half drunk at the time and didn't attach any importance to what she was saying.

Later that night, he put the tape in the video player and nearly passed out from shock at what he saw. When he went into Roxellana's room, fortified by several double shots of whiskey on top of his usual allotment of beer, he was fearful and uncertain of himself. He shook her shoulder.

"Whaa?" she said, full of sleep.

"Why'd you do it?" he slurred, wobbily.

"Do what?" she said, sitting up, shaking her hair out of her eyes.

"Youuu know," he whimpered.

"You're drunk," Roxellana said, disgusted at this new display of weakness and angry at having been awakened.

"Why d' you hate me," he sobbed, unsteady.

She turned over in bed and ignored him. He stayed on for a time, weakly shaking her by the shoulder and demanding that she talk with him, but she wouldn't. Finally, he sat down on the floor, his back to the bed, tears running down his face, and then crawled out of the room. Roxellana rolled over and breathed a sigh of relief.

After that night, Oscar seemed to grow old before everyone's eyes. He sank into a deep depression. He missed work and he could barely get out of bed, but the one thing he insisted on doing was buying Roxellana a car. It didn't make sense. He seemed to be sick and dying, but he was hell bent on spending money they didn't have on a car they swore they would never buy.

That summer Roxellana applied to a few colleges and worked at two part-time jobs. In September she moved into a dorm room on campus at the University of Pittsburgh. She had been in school less than a month when her father shot himself to death. He left no note and no one could figure out what had happened.

Chapter 3

Eric Calder was a lanky kid who worked as a dog handler for Thomas Ilford. Ilford was Pittsburgh's most well-diversified hoodlum. He organized dogfights, sold dope, and ran numbers. Eric lived and worked in a run-down house Ilford had bought him in the East Liberty area.

Three of Ilford's large Pit Bulls lived with him in the house, and he trained them in the fenced-in back yard. Once a month, sometimes twice, he would take the dogs to a fight, work with them in the fighting ring, then, after the fight, patch them up and take them home until the next fight. As long as the dogs won their fights and he got them there on time, no one interfered with him. He liked his job.

Eric lived with a girl he had known in high school named Celeste Bellman. She was a skinny girl, somewhat unattractive, and like Eric, a person who flew underneath the radar. Celeste was a drifter, without direction, marking time, living with Eric because she had nowhere else to live. She liked Eric and the two got along very well. They were lovers, but neither was in love. Living together was just something they did. It was a way through life right then.

Eric was close to the dogs. He had three of them in the house with him. Three big Pit Bulls. The dogs were gentle around Eric and Celeste, but around other dogs, they were killing machines. Eric trained them daily, both to respond to commands and also to kill. Daily, he fed each of them a live bird, or cat, or puppy, and the dogs killed whatever he put in front of them. It was how they learned to kill and how they learned to be aggressive in the ring with other dogs.

When the dogs got hurt in the fights, as they did at almost every match, he and a makeshift medic, Sledge, another kid about Eric's age, plied the bloody gladiatorial dog with antibiotics, bandages, and sometimes leg splints. The dogs got the best that unlicensed veterinarian care could provide. And the dogs knew that Eric and his friend, Sledge, were helping them. They would often turn around and lick Sledge's face as he sponged their wounds. He just laughed and said, "Calm down, Killer. This won't hurt much."

Eric loved the life. He liked the excitement of the fights, the dogs, and the feeling of living on the edge of things. Celeste was less enthralled. She worried that dog fighting was illegal and that Ilford was a criminal. She fantasized that men with guns came and killed them for the dogs, or that they killed the dogs and the people, or that Ilford killed them. It didn't matter who killed who. She didn't like it. Most of the time, she was scared, on edge. And when Eric fed the dogs sacrificial kittens or puppies that were delivered every day, she had to leave the house. Sometimes at night she would imagine the growling of the killer dogs and the screaming of the puppies or kittens as the dogs grabbed them, shook their huge heads until the poor animals were disoriented and half dead, and then killed them with a decisive bite. Sometimes, when she came back too early, Eric would not have had time to hose down the concrete pad in back, and blood would be spattered everywhere.

The killing of the sacrificial animals was a source of tension between them, and gradually it got worse. Sometimes, she wouldn't speak to him for a few days because she was so upset about it. It was during one of these periods of high tension when Eric met Roxellana at a neighborhood bar. She seemed interested in him and Eric liked her. He was starved for female companionship that wasn't judgmental. He longed for someone who could just accept what life was.

Eric didn't like killing the puppies either, but that was what it took to train the dogs to fight and to kill, so that's what he had to do. He couldn't understand why Celeste didn't see that. They had a good life where they were and she just didn't seem to like it. Maybe she didn't like him. People left them alone, they had their own house, Neither one of them had to work, and they had enough money to buy food, go to the bars now and then, and run an old truck. What was not to like?

The tension between Eric and Celeste continued to grow, and when Eric went to the bar every Friday night he began looking at other women. It was there he saw Roxellana. As Celeste's judgmental nastiness seemed to grow and Eric's longing for female companionship intensified, he gradually screwed up his courage and asked Roxellana if he could buy her a drink. It was a long shot. But she accepted and seemed glad to talk to him.

Eric liked the way she looked, with her wide hips and large chest. Eric knew, though, that this relationship wasn't going anywhere because Roxellana was a college girl and Eric was a kid from the wrong side of the tracks. No college girl had ever paid any attention to him before.

But much to his surprise, as time went on, it became clear that Roxellana didn't seem to care about Eric's educational or economic background. She treated him like a man. She wasn't judgmental.

"You're such an interesting guy, Eric," Roxellana said. "I'll bet you're really good at what you do." She had a wide peasant face, long thick hair, and long and well-formed legs. Her breasts were large and Eric couldn't help noticing that her nipples were erect.

"Well, being a dog trainer isn't much of a job," he said.

"Tell me about it," she teased, making a pouting face intended to be seductive. It was the face she made automatically after six or eight beers. She had her father's taste for beer.

"Well. I train and take care of dogs, usually Pit Bulls that are used in dogfights. It's the best job I ever had. I get a place to live and I don't answer to nobody, really, and I like the dogs."

"Are the dogs dangerous?"

"Not for the people they live with," Eric said. "Mostly, they're just dangerous to other dogs."

"What's it like, these dogfights?" Roxellana asked.

"Well, I bring the dogs to the fight and I stay with 'em. Before the fight, the dogs get weighed and then I wash the other guy's dog to make sure he hasn't put any poison on it that will hurt my dog, and he washes my dog," Eric said.

"Poison?"

"Yeah, some of these guys, they use poison. They'll even try to put it on their dog's teeth when they give him a drink, so we have to watch them all the time."

"Wow. And you've got to deal with all of that?"

"It's not such a big deal."

"What happens after you make sure there's no poison?"

"Well, I get in the ring with my dog. It's a ring about twenty feet across. There's a scratch line in the middle. There's also a referee and a timekeeper. I stand with the dog's head and shoulders between my legs, and when the referee says "Let go," I tell the dog to attack."

"Does he?"

"Oh, hell yeah. That's what we train him for."

"Then what?"

"If one of the dogs turns his head and shoulders away from the other dog, it's called a turn and the referee makes the dogs go back to their starting places. The handlers take them back. Then when the referee says "Let go," the dog that turned has to be the first across the scratch line and he has to mouth the other dog or he loses," Eric said.

"Is that it?"

"There's a lot of other stuff, too, like what happens if the dogs don't turn but they also don't fight. But basically, yeah, that's it."

"Do the dogs get hurt?"

"Well, yeah. I've had dogs so chewed up that I just kill em with a .22 bullet to the head. A lot of guys just leave these dogs to die, just thrown 'em out in a field, but I kill 'em. I'd want someone to do that for me if I was a dog," Eric said.

"What if they're just hurt and you don't want to kill them?"

"Then I get Sledge — he's the vet — to bandage 'em up as best he can. Sledge's not really a vet, but he's taught himself how to fix dogs, and he's pretty good at it. He comes to all the fights and Mr. Ilford, he pays him to be there. He gives 'em penicillin and all that shit," Eric said.

"You got a girlfriend?" Roxellana said, the pouting seduction in full swing, rubbing Eric's thigh.

Eric paused, a little uneasy at this turn of the conversation. He stammered a little. “There’s a girl that stays with me sometimes,” Eric evaded, almost whispering.

“Well, why don’t you have me over some time when she isn’t there,” Roxellana said.

Roxellana’s long, tangled, thick auburn hair, her broad peasant face, her forty-two inch chest with matching hips, and her shapely legs, made her the most beautiful woman in the world to Eric. The fact that she was also starting to have a little pot belly which stuck out under her loose blouse was just more of her charm. Eric was thin, six feet, a hundred forty pounds, with a thirty inch waist and narrow shoulders. His long blonde hair covered his ears and acne had broken out along his nose. His face was thin, like his body, and the long hair made him look almost girl-like.

Eric couldn’t resist Roxellana, and by the time Celeste caught Roxellana and Eric in bed together, he was completely under her spell. Celeste moved out, and Roxellana moved in, and she fucked the gangly Eric until he couldn’t take any more. Eric helped her move her belongings out of a dorm room she had been sharing with three other roommates and into his house in the East Liberty section of Pittsburgh.

Chapter 4

Three months before Roxellana met Eric, when her father killed himself, the car payments and her allowance stopped. That's when she began to look around for another source of income and to think about how she was going to survive.

By the time Roxellana moved into the dorm, she had already gone beyond the stage of being the obstreperous school girl who wanted money and a car and freedom to sleep-over with her outrageous boyfriend. Roxellana progressed to the stage of wanting to be free and independent of anyone — parents, boyfriends, teachers, friends — anyone. She wanted to express herself, her developing awareness of her own power as a person and an actor. As an adult.

Roxellana sensed that she was different than the girls she lived with. They too rejected the restrictions that their parents had put on them in high school, and they too flaunted their sexuality in an almost rebellious way. But Roxellana realized that her development involved more than rebellion. She was forging an identity that would give her influence and money.

When Roxellana was midway through the first semester at the university, she had mapped out a four-part plan for success: identify the target; lift your skirt, fuck the target, and take his money. Beautifully simple. No nine-to-five job; no overbearing bosses; no rush hour traffic; no scrambling to pay the bills; no crackerbox house in the suburbs; no husband working the local bank, like her father, and barely making enough money to get along. That was for the suckers. Roxellana was on her own now and she was on a roll.

Roxellana's first trial run of her theory of how to succeed in life without really working involved one Joseph Inverlock. He was her English professor. She had been pursuing Inverlock all semester, and for the most part, he seemed impervious to her not-so-subtle advances, but when she sat in the front row with a short skirt, she noticed he couldn't keep his eyes off her legs.

She did some research on Inverlock and found that he was a forty-two year old associate professor with a Ph.D. from Cornell, two published articles, and according to the faculty handbook, he was researching for a book on the link between Edwardian novels and novels of the eighteenth century. He was up for tenure in a few years.

In class, Inverlock seemed well-organized and at least halfway interesting. He didn't encourage much discussion, preferring instead to lecture from an old notebook which he brought with him to each class. He affected the traditional tweed jackets and wrinkled pants favored by academics. Sometimes he wore a striped tie; others a turtleneck sweater under the jacket.

Roxellana made sure to always sit in the front row of the lecture hall. There was nothing between her and the professor, and she experimented with little moves that seemed to get his attention. Some days, she crossed her legs and pulled her skirt halfway up her thighs. That always got his attention. She tried slacks, but that seemed to be less effective, although she did catch him watching her ass when she left class. Finally, she tried pulling her skirt up and making slight thrusting motions with her hips. That really got his attention, so she made sure to go up and engage in a little meaningless patter after class. And after that, she would go up and talk to Inverlock almost every day after class.

After four or five weeks, Inverlock seemed more relaxed when she approached him, and recently, he had even begun making a few little jokes when they talked. Finally, she scheduled a conference with him about her term paper.

Inverlock's office was located on the sixth floor of the Cathedral of Learning, the University of Pittsburgh's central building. She had dressed carefully for this meeting and she was geared up. When Roxellana knocked on Inverlock's door, she was wearing a very short plaid skirt which came three quarters of the way up her shapely thighs and a tight cotton turtleneck with no bra. As she stepped into Inverlock's office, he looked up and found himself staring at her chest. Roxellana's very large nipples were visible through the shirt. A lump formed in his throat, and he said, "Please, Miss Jameson, come in."

Inverlock was about six feet tall, two hundred pounds, and with a long, horse-like face. Some of the students made fun of the horse-prof behind his back, but Roxellana found it kind of sexy. Inverlock reminded her of one of those Greek mythic figures, half horse half man, who came down from the heavens periodically and fucked poor unsuspecting earth women.

Roxellana sat on a wooden armchair facing him. She crossed her legs, and lowered her books to the floor. Straightening in the chair, she said, demurely, "I rather thought that was for you."

"What?" he said, in distraction.

"Coming in. Aren't you the one who should be coming in?" Her tongue traced the oval of her lips.

Inverlock's face colored slightly, and he got up, walked to the door, and turned the latch.

"Ahhhh," he began. "I think we had better get off on the right foot here, Miss Jameson. You are a very attractive..."

"Shut up, Joey," Roxellana cooed.

"Ahhhh, what do you mean, Miss Jameson?"

"I think you know what I mean."

"Ahhh, Ahhh, no. No. Ahhh, Miss Jameson. I don't believe this is happening. Ahhh..."

At this point, Roxellana, still sitting in the armchair, hiked up her skirt and spread her legs wide apart locking them on the arms of the chair. She was wearing very thin thong panties which could not conceal her labia, the cheeks of her large ass showing underneath, and pubic hair sticking out from the edge of the panties.

Inverlock's eyes were riveted on her vagina, and the lump in his throat threatened to rival the lump in his pants.

"That's better," she whispered. "I know you like the way I look. I've been thinking about this for a long time."

She lowered her legs, stood, pulled her turtleneck over her head, her breasts flopping perkily as she pulled the shirt loose, and undid a pin on the waistband of her skirt, which slipped to the floor, leaving Roxellana standing three feet from Inverlock in her thong panties. Inverlock sat down, his eyes sliding back and forth over her shapely body.

"Oh my God," he said. "You need to get dressed right now."

"We're way beyond that, Joey," she whispered, coming closer and reaching over to smooth his hair, and in the process, putting her breast in his face. He couldn't help himself, and he reached up to touch her breast. It was silky smooth and round, and he felt the erect nipple.

"I shouldn't be doing this," he whimpered.

"It's all right, Joey," she said. "No one has to know. I know you want to. You're really gonna like this."

He touched her stomach and then his hands ran up to her breasts, fondling them and then back down to her wide hips. She started unbuttoning his shirt and threw his tie on the floor. When his shirt was off, she pulled him up by his belt and unfastened the belt and the pants. She knelt expertly down, pulling the pants down as she knelt, and as he stood there with his pants around his ankles, she pulled his jockey shorts down over his erect cock.

"That's a big one, Joey," she cooed, taking it in her mouth and stroking the shaft with one hand.

"Oh, God, don't, I'll come," he said.

Roxellana freed his cock and removed his pants from his legs. She pushed aside all the papers and books on his desk, flinging everything on the floor. She slipped out of her thong panties, hoisted her ample rear end up on the desk and spread her legs wide. The lips of her pussy were warm and inviting. He came forward tentatively, his mouth dry, his lips suddenly parched. He was fearful and yet compelled, and his cock, seeming to have a mind of its own, touched her. He began to ease it in, and she moved her ass to accommodate his angle of entry, gyrating slightly as the tip of his cock played with the wet lips of her vagina. Then, as the tip snuggled in an inch or so, he plunged in and she pulled him into her as deep as he could go. When he reached orgasm, it seemed to both of them that the desk had lifted off the floor.

"Jesus," he said. "Jesus."

"Oh, Joey, that was so good," she whispered.

Over the next weeks, Joey fucked her in the library, in the stacks with her ass wedged against a row of novels, in a library carol with Roxellana leaning forward over a chair, and in the back seat of his car. Now and then, he'd take her in the bushes of Schenley Park.

By the time Thanksgiving came, Roxellana persuaded Inverlock to come to her room in the dorm. Everyone would be gone, she explained, and they would have a real bed.

Inverlock came to the room reluctantly, slinking through the halls, and hurriedly slipped into Roxellana's room.

"You're silly," she said. "I told you. No one is here. It's just you and me."

She was dressed in thong panties and nothing else. He lost no time in getting out of his clothes, except that his stiff cock made it difficult to get out of his pants. By the time he was undressed, Roxellana was on the bed with her legs spread wide, and welcoming arms held up to receive him. He came to her gratefully and fucked her as if it was his last act on earth.

A video camera hummed away in a shelf of books, unseen.

• • •

Afterwards, at a restaurant in Oakland, Roxellana said, "Joey, I think I love you."

"Love is a very complicated thing," he said, uneasily.

"I know. You think I don't know?"

"Well, it's just that you're so young."

"I guess I'm old enough to fuck," she teased, enjoying his discomfort.

"No, I... I just mean that you will meet a lot of people in your life..."

"So what?"

"Well, you may find that you love one of them more than you think you love me."

"Why don't we worry about that when it happens," she smiled, lighting a cigarette.

"I didn't know you smoked," he said.

"Don't change the subject, Joey. We were talking about love."

"Oh, yes... Love."

"Are you saying you don't love me?"

"No. Of course not."

"Well, you're not saying you *do* love me, either," she said.

He looked at her and said, "Roxellana, I love you, but you know I'm married. This can never work."

"Why can't it work?" she said.

"I'm too old for you," he said.

"Is your wife better in bed than I am?" she said.

"No. It's not that," he said.

"What then?"

"You're a student. I'm a professor. That won't work."

"Seems like it works to me," she said.

"It's not just about sex," he said.

"What is it about?"

"I don't know, Roxellana. It just can't work."

"But it is working."

"We have to be very careful. We have to make sure no one knows."

"Are you ashamed of me?"

"No. You're beautiful. I would be proud to be with you."

"Then why not be with me?"

"I'd lose my family. My job. My friends. I'd lose everything."

"We'd have each other," she smiled.

"I know we would. But don't you see, I just can't lose everything I've worked for."

"So it's all about you, then?"

"No, no, I didn't mean that."

"That's what you said."

"I didn't mean to say that."

"Do you want to stop seeing me?"

"God, no. I want to see you always. You know that."

Chapter 5

"I want to see you always," he had said. She could hear him saying it. Problem was he didn't mean it. He was sticking with the wife. In some ways it was a disappointment. It would have been kind of fun to strut around the campus as Professor Inverlock's mistress, the woman he had left his wife for. The woman of his dreams, and, in all probability, she thought, of every professor's dreams.

She was going to miss that. But after all, it was finally about money. If Joey wanted to pay her by living with her and showing her off, that was fine. If not, he would have to just pay her. Just like her father had paid her. She didn't care, really, because the object was money. The rest of it was just fluff. So after the Thanksgiving fling, she allowed Inverlock to fuck her now and then, just to keep him on the line and to make sure he had made up his mind about leaving his wife. But then she moved in with Eric and left Inverlock to his own devices.

Roxellana came up behind Eric as he read the paper, and started rubbing his shoulders. She could feel the knots.

"Eric," she said, "I really like it here. I like living with you."

"Me too," Eric said, glancing up from the paper.

"I think it's really neat we get along so well," she said.

"Yeah, I really like it," he said.

There was a pause while she kneaded his shoulders, and then she sad, "Eric..."

"Yeahhhh," he said absentmindedly, continuing to read.

"I need some money."

Eric continued reading. "I don't have any money. You know that, Roxellana. You've seen my checkbook." Eric said.

"I know," she said. "I'm not asking you for money. I only need your help in getting some money."

"What do you need money for, anyway?" he said, turning pages.

"I need money for school. I got to pay tuition and buy books. And I got a car payment, and other stuff."

"How did you do all that before?"

"I had some money saved up and I got money from home."

"Can't you ask for money from home again?"

"No. It stopped."

"Why?"

"Listen to me, Eric. It' not important why. It just stopped. But I have a way to get some money. I really need your help."

There was an urgency in her voice that got his attention now, and he put the paper down. She came around in front of him and knelt down touching his knees and looking mournful.

"Okay I'll help you if I can. What do you want me to do?"

"Before I met you," she began, hesitantly, "I had been going out with one of my professors."

"Really?"

"Yeah."

"Wow."

"But he's married."

"Oh. Did you know that?"

"Yeah."

"You thought he'd leave his wife?"

"No."

"Then why'd you do it?"

"Because I could see the time coming when I'd need money."

"And you thought he would lend you what you needed?"

"No. I thought he would give me what I asked for."

"What if his wife found out?"

"That's why he would give me what I asked for. So she wouldn't find out."

"Jesus. You mean you were blackmailing him?"

"Wel... yeah. I still am."

"You're blackmailing him?" Eric said, disbelieving.

"Yeah."

"How much has he paid you?"

"Nothing. Yet. He's going to make the first payment soon. I just told him."

"What if he doesn't pay and you tell the wife, but the wife doesn't believe you."

"She'd likely believe a video tape, don't you think?"

"You taped him and you having sex?"

"Yeah."

"Jesus, Roxellana. That's some dangerous shit."

"He's just an academic, Eric. He's a fucking professor, for Christ's sake. It's not like he was dangerous," she said impatiently.

"So what are you going to do?"

"I already asked him for ten thousand dollars. Now I'm going to call him and tell him that I want him to deliver the money here."

"Ten thousand dollars? And what if he tells you to get lost?"

"His wife gets the tape."

"Has he seen the tape?"

"I sent it to him last week."

"Has he tried to talk to you."

"He doesn't know where I am. Remember. I moved out of my old dorm room and I've been skipping class."

"Jesus, Roxellana. I don't know about this. You're fucking with some dangerous shit."

"Eric, here's all you have to do. I'm going to have him come over here tomorrow to pay me the money. All you have to do is be here so he doesn't get rough with me. He'll see somebody else is here and he won't be difficult."

"You said he's a wimp."

"I didn't say he's a wimp, but he probably is. He's not going to cause any trouble. You're just here to make sure. Okay?"

"I don't know, Roxellana. I don't like it. How'd you think this up anyway?"

"I've done it before."

"What?"

"Yeah. It works great. You show 'em the tape and they pay you money. Just like a charm."

"How do you know that? You mean you go around the country fucking people and making tapes of it?"

"No. I just did it once before."

"Who did you do it to?"

"You don't want to know."

"I do want to know. Maybe it would work there but not here."

"It will work."

"Who? Goddam it. Who?"

"My father."

"What?"

"My father. You wanted to know. My father. Goddam it."

"You did this to your father? You fucked your father and put it on tape? What?"

"My father was a drunk. He couldn't remember what happened from one night to the next. So I just waited until he got drunk and then I fucked him," Roxellana answered. "He didn't even remember it. Even after I showed him the tape. He couldn't believe it."

"Neither can I. Why did you do it?"

"I 'd been asking the bastard for a car and more money and the freedom to come and go as I pleased, and I wasn't getting it," she said.

"So you fucked him and put it on tape, and what did he do?"

"He bought me the car and gave me a big allowance and I came and went as I pleased. My mother went nuts because of his giving me all this stuff and things got pretty tense for a while."

"So you blackmailed him and he paid."

"Yeah."

"But he's not paying anymore. So it doesn't really work, then, does it?"

"Yeah, it works."

"How so? He stopped paying. It doesn't work."

"He paid right up until he died."

"What happened?"

"He killed himself."

"He what?" the boy erupted.

"Yeah," she said, "He shot himself to death. In a parking lot. It was pretty dumb."

"It was dumb? That's all you can say?" the boy said, agitated, dropping the newspaper on the floor and staring at her with intense disbelief.

"What do you want me to do Eric? He's dead. I didn't kill him. He killed himself."

"Jesus, Roxellana, you killed him as sure as if you'd shot him."

Sensing that things were going badly, Roxellana turned to the boy, put her arms around him and said sweetly, "Oh Eric, you're so wonderful. Let's don't ruin it with this. I didn't kill him. You can see that. We need to think about us."

"When did all this happen?" he said.

"A few months ago," she said.

"What did you do when you found out?"

"Nothing. What would I do? I'm in school. I went to the funeral, that's all."

"What did your mom say?"

"What do you think? She was all broken up. He supported her. Now she has to work."

"That's it?"

"He was no great dad and no great husband, Eric. He was a fucking drunk who told himself stories about how our life was. She's better off without him. I think she even sees that now."

"I can't believe you did that to your own father," Eric said.

"Let's change the subject, do you mind?

"Yeah? Like what? Like how we're gonna deal with this guy when he comes over here to blow your head off instead of paying you the money?"

"He's not gonna blow my head off, Eric."

"Right. He's gonna blow my head off."

Chapter 6

A week later, Eric sat in the living room reading the paper. He heard steps on the porch, then a pounding on the door. It was not a friendly pounding. Eric looked up from his newspaper and saw a man's form through the opaque blinds on the window of the door. He was about to call Roxellana when she appeared in the doorway to the kitchen, already on her way to answer the door. The pounding started again. She opened the door.

"Hello, slut," the man said as soon as Roxellana's face became visible at the open door.

Roxellana put her hand against the man's chest and pushed him back out onto the front porch, following him out and closing the door behind her.

"Who the fuck's in there?" the man shouted. "You think you can just do this to me? Ruin my life and stand there with a fucking smirk on your face?"

"Joey," Roxellana cooed, "calm down, I've never seen you like this."

"Well, I was just getting started. Who the hell do you think you are, anyway? Did you think I would just roll over and give you all my money? You sandbag me. You use my feelings for you to work me over like some mark. Is that all I was to you? Some John?"

Eric decided this wasn't going the way Roxellana had thought it would. He could hear that the professor was getting more and more excited, and from the sound of the thuds against the living room wall, he was banging Roxellana up against the side of the house. Eric went into the bedroom and called Ilford's numbers operation, which was located in Bloomfield, two miles away. There was more shouting and scuffling on the porch.

"Hello, this is Eric. I'm Mr. Ilford's dog guy. I raise his Pitt Bulls. I need some help here. There's some nut pounding on the door, says he's gonna kill the dogs. You better get somebody over here right away."

"Where you at, kid, that house in East Liberty?" Ilford's goon asked.

"Yeah."

"Hold on kid, we'll be right there."

As Eric walked back into the living room, he could hear that the yelling on the porch had escalated and he began looking around for something to use as a club. He was going to have to go out there before Roxellana got killed. This guy wasn't your mild mannered professor.

Before Eric could act, the door burst open and the tall man on the porch pushed Roxellana, stumbling backwards, into the room. The man stepped into the room, his face red and angry. He pushed her again, and she stumbled backwards and fell onto the couch, which was behind her against the wall. The man stood in the middle of the room, the door still open, staring at Eric.

"Who the fuck are you?" he spat at Eric.

"I live here."

"With the slut?"

"Yeah."

"So you two think you can just rob me and ruin my life?"

"Look, mister, I don't know what you're talking about," Eric stammered.

"Sit down, kid. You're in this up to your eyeballs, so don't fuck with me," he said.

Eric sat down next to Roxellana.

"Where are all the tapes? You give them to me and I'll walk out of here. But if you don't, I got nothing to lose, and I'll hurt both of you."

"Come on, Mister..."

"Shut up."

"There was only one tape, Joey," Roxellana said.

"Yeah, and I'm the Pope," the angry man said.

"Really, Joey," she said.

He walked up to the girl, grabbed her by the collar of her shirt, and spat in her face, "Give me the tapes."

Eric leaned over and grabbed the professor's arm, trying to release Roxellana from the enraged man's grip, but the professor backhanded him and knocked him to the end of sofa.

"You sit there, boy. And you come with me, bitch," he said, pulling Roxellana up by the front of her shirt. The professor was anything but the calm professional man. He was the enraged beast fighting for what he thought was his life. If the tape surfaced, he could kiss his career and his family good bye.

The professor pushed Roxellana ahead of him to the chest of drawers which was sitting by the wall. Holding onto Roxellana's shirtfront with one hand, he pulled out the drawers one at a time and threw their contents all over the room. When the contents of the last drawer were strewn over the living room floor, he shouted in her face, "Tell me where it is."

"There is no tape, Joey. You have the only one. I told you," she said.

He pushed her into the bedroom and Eric could hear the sound of drawers being pulled from chests and hitting the floor. All the while, he yelled for her to tell him where the tapes were and she pleaded with him that there were no more tapes.

When the professor had finished with the bedroom, he pushed Roxellana back through the door to the living room, and she tripped on the debris on the floor, sprawling on her hands and knees.

As Roxellana lay on the floor with Eric looking on frightened from the couch, the front door flew open as if it had been hit by a gust from a tornado and slammed into the wall knocking plaster loose. A man too big to fit through the door stood in the doorway. He hunched down and peered into the room. Roxellana was on the floor, Eric was on the couch, and the professor stood in the bedroom door. The man too big for the opening bent his knees and stepped sideways through the door. Once into the room, he kicked the empty drawers littering the floor out of his way. His head nearly brushed the ceiling. He stood towering over Roxellana for a second, sized up the professor as the aggressor, and said, "What the fuck?"

"That's him," Eric said, pointing at the professor.

"Who are you?" the professor said to the enormous man, amazed at his sheer size. Involuntarily, the professor found himself shrinking back into the bedroom.

Two other men, much smaller but with faces that looked like lumps of metal beaten with hammers, came in behind the big man and stood on either side of the door. The big man said nothing, but stepped purposefully toward the professor, who immediately backed up into the bedroom. The giant dipped sideways after him into the bedroom and within seconds, the professor came flying out the door, sprawling on the floor where Roxellana had been earlier.

"Wait a minute," the professor pleaded, now clearly frightened out of his wits. "We can talk about this. Call them off," he pleaded to Roxellana. "I don't know who these guys are, but we can talk about this. I can pay. I, I, I just didn't know how serious you were about this. Come on, goddam it Roxellana, I mean it, call this guy off. This is something we can talk about. I told you, I can pay. I can pay."

The men, Ilford's muscle, didn't even know who Roxellana was, and were not, in any case, taking anyone's counsel but their own.

The giant emerged from the bedroom and again walked directly to Joey, who was now scooting backwards frantically across the debris strewn floor, trying to escape the grasping hands of the big man.

"Call him off, Roxellana. Call him off. I take it back. I'll pay whatever you want," he pleaded, sobbing hysterically, as he crawled and stumbled across the floor.

But the giant caught up to him and grabbed him by the belt, then lifted him over his head. The professor hung helplessly in the air, his arms and legs flailing. He screamed for Roxellana to help him. But Roxellana couldn't help him. She and Eric watched, transfixed, as the giant held Joey against the ceiling, and then, in a moment of terror, slammed him down onto a coffee table. The table, except for its steel frame, collapsed into splinters. The loud crack was Joey's spine snapping in two as it bent backwards over the frame of the table. His body fell limp on the wreckage.

The giant looked at the motionless figure, kicked the lifeless body to see if there was any reaction. There was none, and he walked to the front door, stepped sideways, and left the house. The two hammer-forged-face men bent to pick up the body.

As the two men carried the body of the professor toward the door, one of them turned. "Yun'z didn't see nothin," he said. "And if ya think ya did, y'll end up just like this."

A week later, the broken body of Professor Joseph Inverlok was found in woods alongside Frank Curto Park on Bigelow Boulevard. All the major organs of his body shut down when his spinal cord was severed.

Chapter 7

Two weeks later, a Mercedes S 600 pulled up to the curb in front of a large four-story brick house on Pacific Avenue in the Bloomfield section of Pittsburgh. It was the residence of Sam Budda, Nick Savarese, and Maria Llanas. The three were partners in a personal protection business.

The V12 engine was so quiet that it would be difficult to tell whether the driver turned it off before he got out, or left the car running. Dark windows obscured the back seat of the large sedan, but in the front, there was a driver and a large person with long blonde hair pulled back in a pony tail. Pony tail was out of the car and waiting watchfully at the curb for the driver to open the rear passenger's door. The figure with the pony tail was apparently a man, but actually, it was a woman built like an armored personnel carrier and dressed in a man's suit. She stood over six feet tall. The driver opened the rear door next to the curb and a gray haired man got out. The man, followed closely by the large woman, walked to the front door. The driver stood by the car.

The man leading the way was in his sixties, impeccably dressed in a blue pin striped suit, white shirt, Nordic blue plain tie, a Borsolino fedora, and black oxfords that rivaled the Mercedes for sheer brilliance of shine. The large woman stood to the side while the gray haired man pushed the doorbell, her gaze scanning the street, the house, and the neighboring yards.

Sam Budda answered the door. The dark Mitch Rosen gunbelt barely concealed a jumbo Demko folding knife inside the waistband.

"Mr. Budda? I'm Nathan Inverlok."

"Yes, good to see you. Please, come in."

"I assume you have no objection if my assistant, Gabriella, comes along," Inverlok said.

"Your assistant is welcome," Sam said. "This way."

Gabriella followed her employer inside and Sam closed the front door. "I've seen this woman somewhere before," Sam thought. "I just can't place her."

"This is a very attractive house," Inverlok said.

"Thanks, we've spent a fair amount of time on it," Sam said, taking the lead into the foyer.

The two men stood in a central foyer facing inward, toward the back of the house. To the right was the dining room, straight ahead were stairs to the second floor, and to the left was an arch leading to an oversized living room, which had been formed by removing a wall between two separate living rooms, one behind the other, in the original house.

On the floor of the living room was a large oriental rug, fifteen feet by twenty- six feet, which sat in the middle of the room.

"That is the most striking Isfahan I have ever seen," Inverlok said. "It's beautiful."

The rug had a large vermillion field with a central sixteen pointed stylized star in a soft gold, and throughout the field were blue, green, tan and ivory flowers.

"Yes, it's one of my favorites," Sam said.

"I'm not usually fond of Isfahans because they seem gaudy," Inverlok said.

"I know what you mean," Sam said. "I think it's the coloration that makes this one attractive as much as anything. Some of them have too much white, apparently attempting to mimic the coloring of the mosques. But that doesn't work for the Western eye."

"I think you've put your finger on it," Inverlok said.

"Come in and have a seat," Sam said.

Inverlok sat in an Eames chair and Sam sat opposite him a Scandinavian reclining swivel chair. Gabriella stood ten yards behind her employer in a corner, back to the wall, eyes watchful.

"Can I offer you tea?," Sam said. The tea set was on the table between them, the pot under a thick cozy.

"Thanks, yes," Inverlok said. Sam poured two cups from an iron Japanese pot and handed one to Inverlok. The cup and saucer were Packard china in white with gold trim.

Inverlock was of fair complexion, about five-nine or five-ten, and trim, maybe a hundred seventy pounds. His face was refined, and yet, purposeful. The features were even, balanced. The gray hair was thick and hung over his ears slightly. If there was a single distinguishing feature in the refined face it was his mouth, which was wide and almost sensuous.

Interlock smiled, appraising the man opposite him and continuing to size up Sam's house as he sipped his tea.

Sam saw Inverlok's eyes scanning the room in a practiced manner, assessing what and who he was dealing with. As he scanned the far wall of bookshelves, his eyes stopped, he put his tea cup down and he sat up straight in his chair.

"Is that a bear?" Inverlok said, marveling at his own question, and staring at the reclining figure of a hundred and fifty pound Akita, silently lying across the room from Inverlok and watching the newcomers intently for signs of bad behavior.

"It's just my dog," Sam said. "His name is Ronin."

"Why is he so quiet, just lying there?"

"Akitas are hunters. Ronin is silent and watches."

"You mean he's stalking me?"

"You could say that, I suppose, but actually what he's doing is just watching what is going on to make sure there is no threat to me."

"You say he is silent. Doesn't he bark?"

"Only when there is danger."

"I don't think I have ever seen a dog that looks more like a bear. Is he friendly?"

"Would you like to meet him?"

"I don't know. Is it safe?"

"Ronin. Come."

Ronin got up from his bed and slowly walked into the center of the room. He stood beside Sam and looked coolly at Inverlok and at Gabriella, ten yards distant. Gabriella shifted slightly to the left.

"It's Okay," Sam said to Ronin.

Ronin understood. He walked three steps over to Inverlok's chair and put his basketball sized head on the man's knee. Gingerly, Inverlok touched the thick fur on the top of Ronin's head and said, "Good boy." Ronin's tail began to wag, just slightly.

"He likes you," Sam said.

"How do you know that?" Inverlok said.

"He didn't remove your leg," Sam said.

Inverlok looked at Sam, a slight fear in his eyes.

"No, just kidding," Sam laughed. "His tail wagged. He likes you."

"Thank god," Inverlok said. "He's the most beautiful dog I've ever seen."

"That's what most people say," Sam said. "But don't say it too often. It goes to his head and then he's difficult."

Both men smiled and Ronin walked a short distance away, then lay down between them, facing Inverlok. He put his huge head between his paws and closed his eyes in complete trust and confidence. This was a friend, and in any case, Sam was watching his back.

Inverlok recovered some of his composure and said, "You come highly recommended. I talked with Dan Houston in the White House, and he said that you are trustworthy."

"I'm surprised. Such praise from Houston is an honor. Of course, he's a bit of a maverick, so his judgment may be a bit off," Sam said.

"That's what he said about you," Inverlok laughed. "He said you and your cohort were a highly regarded contractors for the Department of Defense."

"Well," Sam said, "I don't know about highly regarded, but yeah, Nick and I worked for some of those agencies."

"You are modest," Inverlock said.

"What brings you here?" Sam said.

"I lost a son. I guess he was a son," Inverlok said.

"And you want me to find him?"

"No. You can't find him. He's dead. Murdered. I want you to find out who killed him."

Sam paused. "What about the police? They're pretty good at that."

"Not in this case. They have no suspects."

"Where was he killed?"

"Here. In Pittsburgh."

"Do you have any theories?"

"Not really. He and I didn't see eye-to-eye. We didn't talk much. I didn't know much about his life. He was married and has — had — a small child is all I know. Oh, and he worked at the university."

"The University of Pittsburgh?"

"Yes."

"What did he teach?"

"Something called communications."

"But you and he didn't communicate?"

"No."

"Why not?"

"Because he was throwing his life away and I wanted him in the business."

"Why do you say he was throwing his life away?"

"He was a college professor."

"That's throwing his life away?"

"Yes. College professors don't do anything but talk and write horseshit."

"Well, that's true, but couldn't it be said that business tycoons don't do anything but make money and adopt morally superior attitudes?"

"I see you speak your mind."

"That's a habit I have."

"Your point is well taken. I guess it's just that I had always hoped to have a son I could be close to. Someone who shared my dreams. Someone who worked where I worked."

"But in spite of the fact that your son didn't share your dreams, you still care enough about him to come here to see me."

"Who knows why I came here. Maybe I came here because I'm offended someone would kill my son — my son. Maybe I came here because I'm grieving. Maybe I came here to be morally superior one last time — to find the murderer he couldn't protect himself against."

"So your motivation is uncertain. Maybe you should give some more thought to whether you want to pursue this."

"Not really, Mr. Budda. You are right that I am unsure of my exact motivation, but for whatever reasons, I know I want to do this."

"You know my fee."

"Yes. I have a check for you. If you do your job in less time than two months, you and your associate keep the whole amount anyway."

"And what is the job?"

"I would like you and your associate to find out who killed Joseph."

"We give you a name. That is the job?"

"Yes."

"It's possible that at the end of two months we may have nothing to tell you at all. Nick and I will, of course, do our best, but occasionally we draw blank cards. It's a possibility."

"I understand. I am hiring you to do your best. If your best turns up nothing, so be it. I have prepared a written report which includes everything I know about my son, including photographs. That will give you a place to start."

Inverlok stood and placed a thick envelope on the table between them. Ronin stirred and looked at the standing figure. Sam rose, shook his client's hand, and walked him to the front door. Ronin came along behind. At the door, Inverlok turned and rubbed Ronin's ears. The big dog's tail wagged. Gabriella looked at Ronin and smiled at her employer's affinity for dogs. The two men said goodbye and Inverlok, with Gabriella close behind, walked to the

S600. At the car, the driver opened the back door when Inverlok approached. Inverlock disappeared into the shaded safety of the large sedan and Gabriella, having checked the sidewalk in both directions, resumed her place in the passenger side of the front seat. Ronin made a small noise in his throat as the Mercedes glided away from the curb.

Chapter 8

After Inverlok left, Sam called Nick and Maria.

"We got some work," he said. "Come on down for lunch and we'll talk about it."

Nick and Maria lived above Sam in the same large house, and all three units were connected by a back stairway. Sam lived on the first floor; Maria on the second and Nick on the third.

Maria and Nick both arrived in Sam's kitchen by way of the back stairs about noon. Sam had homemade chili, grilled cheese sandwiches and a small salad with feta cheese. Pomegranate juice was the drink.

"Smells great," Maria said.

"Sure does," Nick said.

This living arrangement was ideal. Everyone had his own privacy and each had the security of being close at hand with the others.

The nature of the personal protection business required that they have safe places to stay in the event of trouble. This house, which would be a primary residence, allowed them to stay away from their other safe houses, making them less likely to be compromised. The Pacific Avenue house was owned by Red Sun Holdings, a corporation which was, in turn, owned by another corporation,

Hadrian's Wall, Inc., and Hadrian's Wall, in turn, was owned by The Vanilla Partners, a Panama corporation. This made it difficult to locate any of them by doing a property search.

Sam dished out the chili and the sandwiches, Nick poured the pomegranate juice, and Maria divided the salad. Ronin took up a guard position just inside the kitchen where he could watch both entrances and his masters while they ate lunch.

"I thought we weren't looking for work," Maria said.

"We're not. We don't have to take this job," Sam said, "but I thought I should run it past you. Besides, the guy has already written us a check."

Sam passed the check to Nick and he passed it to Maria. They returned it to Sam without comment.

"People don't write checks — big checks like that — unless they think the job involves the distinct possibility of us getting whacked," Nick said, picking up his sandwich.

"I don't think so. This guy Inverlok, he's some sort of industry mogul, wants us to find out who murdered his son. The son was a professor at Pitt and the police seem to be uninterested, at least according to Inverlok."

"Doesn't sound too dangerous," Nick said.

"That's what you always say," Maria said.

Sam laughed. "Well, I suppose if it wasn't dangerous, he wouldn't be paying us that kind of money. But it doesn't sound any more dangerous that some other things we've done."

"Yeah, you're right about that," Maria said, "except we are dealing with a murder."

"Good point," Sam said. "It's always possible that if we try to put the finger on whoever did it, they'll try to put the finger on us."

"Especially if it's a drug ring, which it sounds like this might be," Nick said. "I don't know what else a professor is likely to get killed for."

"So are we interested or not?" Sam said.

"Why not?" Nick said. "We don't have anything better to do."

"Okay," Maria smiled. "As jobs go, this one sounds pretty tame. Besides, somebody's got to be there to get you two out of trouble."

Chapter 9

"All right, Eric, now what do we do? They killed him. They fuckin killed him. Do you hear me, you idiot, they killed him. He was my meal ticket, and they killed him," Roxellana yelled.

"It was your idea to bring him here," Eric said.

"Yeah, but I didn't know you were gonna call the killers. How the hell would I know that?"

"This guy, Roxellana, he was gonna beat you to a pulp. And me too. He was pissed. He was just getting started. We're lucky the goons got here when they did," Eric said.

"Eric, use your goddam head. He was worth ten thousand dollars to me. Ten thousand, Eric. How the hell am I going to replace that?"

Eric stuck his head back into the newspaper and said, "I guess you'll just have to find another professor."

"Yeah, well it's fine for you to make jokes. You're not the one who is out the money," she snorted.

"Look, Roxellana, I'm sorry it didn't work out, but I wasn't gonna stand here and get beat up by some wild-ass professor just because you think you can shake him down. Yeah, maybe you could, after he beat the shit out of both of us."

"You're pathetic," Roxellana said, walking out of the room in a huff.

• • •

Later that week, Mr. Ilford himself showed up at the East Liberty house. He entered the front door without knocking flanked by three goons and stared at Roxellana, sitting on the couch, her legs curled under her, reading a textbook. Her skirt was pulled up and exposed her well-shaped thighs.

Ilford said, "Who the fuck are you?" The goons watched, alert for threats coming from the stranger.

"I'm Eric's friend."

Ilford's gaze traveled up and down the shapely thighs.

"Where is Eric?" Ilford instinctively put on his I'm-in-charge-here tone to impress the girl.

"He's out back with the dogs."

"Get him."

The girl stood up and seemed to gather some composure when she did. She thrust her chest out a little, her nipples showing against the thin fabric of her t-shirt, and said, "You must be Mr. Ilford. Please, sit on the couch. I'll get him right away. Can I get you something to drink?"

Ilford stared at her appraisingly. This was something he didn't expect. The girl was coming on to him. "Yeah, he said. I'll have some water."

She hustled out of the room and into the kitchen. Ilford could hear the kitchen door slam and voices outside.

Ilford was nearly fifty, balding, six feet tall, twenty five pounds overweight, and overbearing. His big forearms and hands made him forget that he was out of shape. His gray eyes were shaded by bushy eyebrows that seemed to accentuate his baldness, and his well-shaped nose was perched atop a somewhat crooked mouth.

He played golf and squash and did a little swimming. In his role as small-time numbers operator and drug dealer, he occasionally got an upper body workout pounding on some guy's face while his goons held the poor bastard down.

Eric came in closely followed by Roxellana, carrying a glass of water with ice in it. Eric's manner was hesitant, and he hung back in the doorway as Roxellana brushed past him and walked directly to Ilford, standing in front of him with her legs spread apart, then bending at the waist toward him as she handed him the water. The goons watched the newcomer.

"If there's anything else I can get you, Mr. Ilford, please let me know," she purred.

"Sit here, doll," he said, instantly seizing the opportunity and patting the sofa next to him. Then "You, kid, come over here. What the fuck happened here?"

Roxellana sat next to Ilford, allowing her skirt to come midway up her thigh as she crossed her legs. Ilford looked at her legs as he took a sip of water.

"Well, Mr. Ilford," Eric stammered, "I just thought he was gonna do something to the dogs and I called your guys and they came in here and the big guy, he just killed him."

"Who was this guy? The one Tiny killed." Ilford said.

"He was some guy we saw when we were walking the dogs," Roxellana interjected, looking at Ilford, "I think he was a college professor, and the first time we saw him, he started going on about the dogs, how dangerous they were. He followed us home here last week and he said Pit Bulls should be killed."

Ilford looked at Roxellana and then at her thighs crossed for him to appreciate.

"So you saw this guy before today when you walk the dogs. Do you live here too?" Ilford said to Roxellana. "Is that why you were walking the dogs with Eric here?"

"Yes, Mr. Ilford, Eric lets me stay here. I go to college too. And when I'm here, I help him with the dogs," she said

"Why didn't you tell us about this guy before?" Ilford said.

"We didn't think he was serious," Roxellana said. "Then he came pounding on the door and Eric called you while I stalled him."

"Smart girl," Ilford said. Then to Eric, "Do you talk, kid, or does your girlfriend talk for you?"

He looked at Roxellana, checking to see that she appreciated his compliment. She smiled at him, uncrossed her legs, and ran her tongue around the edge of her mouth.

"She's better at talking than I am," Eric said.

"I'll bet you're good at other things too, aren't you?" Ilford said.

"I'll be good at anything you want," Roxellana purred, slightly raising her pelvis as she talked.

"How about you come with me now," Ilford said. "Maybe we can find something for you to do in this operation. You don't mind if I borrow your girlfriend for a while, do you Eric?"

"Oh, No, Mr. Ilford. That's fine."

"I thought it would be," Ilford said, getting up. "Let's go Miss Icewater. What's your name?" turning to look at her again.

"Roxellana."

"Suits you."

"Thanks."

Ilford and Roxellana left, followed by the three heavies. The door closed and Eric was alone.

Outside, one of the goons opened the door of the stretch limousine for Ilford and Roxellana. One goon drove the limousine and the other two followed in another car. Inside, Ilford pushed a button and a dark glass partition went up back of the driver.

Roxellana had her blouse most of the way off by the time the window reached the top, and within seconds after that, she reached behind her back and released the catch on her bra. She shrugged it forward and her soft round boobs fluttered out of the bra, their big nipples pointing lasciviously at Ilford.

"Oh, my," was all he could say.

He helped her out of her skirt and ripped her thong panties off. She straddled him as she unbuckled his pants and pulled them down, with his undershorts. Ilford's erect cock stood up like a telephone pole, and Roxellana grabbed it, rubbing it against the wet lips of her vagina.

"Oh, my yourself," she said, straddling him and easing him in a little at a time, her strong thighs gripping him, and coaxing him up into her.

Ilford guided her ass back and forward and his cock sunk in deeper and deeper a little at a time until he was in all the way and Roxellana was moving her body in ways he could not resist.

Her hips undulated in a circular motion, first to the left, and then to the right. The muscular walls of her vagina gripped the contours of his cock firmly and with a hot lubricity. She moved him first one way, then, the other, circularly and then up and down. Ilford squirmed in ecstasy.

The orgasm came on suddenly and Ilford's head exploded when it did. As far as he could tell, sperm shot clear through the roof of the car. But Roxellana was still there, gripping him strongly and massaging the big cock to do its work. And then the swell built again with the pressure in his head. Roxellana now switched her movements to a new powerful up and down thrust, coaxing again and again until the new orgasm exploded with even more force than before.

Finally, Ilford slumped exhausted, and Roxellana smiled down, a slight dampness of sweat on her upper lip, pleased with her work. He loved it. She had him. She knew she had him now.

Roxellana returned to the East Liberty dog house that evening, but by the next evening, Ilford moved her into an apartment in Shadyside.

After that, Ilford and Roxellana were a number. Ilford saw her every day and took her out to dinner and dancing several times a week. Gradually, he also took her into his confidence. She was smart, not like the bimbos he's been involved with before. She was a college girl.

Over time, her influence became more apparent. Ilford dressed better. His suits were less shiny and his ties were silk. He even started watching what he ate. Salads became de rigueur.

By the time three months had passed, Roxellana had become a familiar face at Ilford's Strip District office, and he had become a familiar figure at her apartment building. Ilford always traveled with two or three heavies, who waited outside in the car when he visited Roxellana. The two seemed to be good for each other. Ilford encouraged Roxellana's studies and she encouraged him in his business operations. She liked the idea of being the girlfriend of a criminal.

Chapter 10

Ilford was loosely known as a crime boss. He ran a numbers operation and supplemented his numbers income with dog fighting and drug dealing. Some of the dogs who fought belonged to Ilford; some belonged to others. He talked openly with Roxellana about his business operations and she was actively interested in them. Often she had suggestions to make, some of which were insightful. She was smart. It was good, she agreed, to run a number of criminal enterprises rather than relying on only one.

Ilford loved smart people, but in his line of work, he didn't get an opportunity to be around intelligence very often. Roxellana was refreshing.

If there was one thing that Ilford was convinced of, it was that conventional behavior was for idiots. His brothers were conventional and he was contemptuous of them. For Ilford smart people thought outside of convention.

Roxellana was nothing if not unconventional and sometimes her lack of convention surprised even Ilford. On one occasion, he mentioned to her that some screwballs in Vas Vegas wanted him to run a dogfight where dogs killed men. The screwballs would then bet on how long it would take to kill each man.

Much to his amazement, Roxellana seized on this idea as a good one. Ilford already had the dogs and the arenas, and they could always pick derelicts up off the street, so start-up costs would be low. But profits would be high. He could charge several thousand dollars a seat for the rubes to come in from Vegas to see the killing, and he could fleece them by taking bets on how long it would take the dogs to kill the man.

At first Ilford rejected the idea. It was ludicrous. Why the hell would he want to kill a bunch of people just to amuse some punk-ass jerks from Las Vegas. But Roxellana persisted. It would be fun, she insisted. And it would be profitable. He could charge a bundle for seats. The rubes would pay it. He began to soften.

For more than three months, Roxellana went with Ilford to the dogfights and never lost a chance to remind him of the money he could make on admissions for the dog-man fights. Besides that, it would make him a big man. No one else had the balls to do something like that.

Finally, she prevailed. They were sitting in a barn near Apollo where Ilford conducted the biggest fights. The crowd had gone and Roxellana pulled Ilford's hand to her.

"Look here, Tommy," she said. "You have it all. You got the dogs and the handlers," pointing to the men, including Eric, loading the scarred wounded Pit Bulls into their cages, "you got the place," pointing to the barn and the bleachers that surrounded them, "and you got me to help you. What more do you need?" she purred.

Ilford had just made a bundle on the fight and was feeling flush. "You're right," he said. "I'll do it."

• • •

A month later, Roxellana kissed Ilford awake and said softly, "Tommy, when is it?"

"When is what?" he mumbled, full of sleep.

"You know. The dogfights you promised me," she said, lifting herself onto her elbows and staring into his face.

"Oh, for Christ's sake." Ilford rolled over to avoid her and said, "Forget it, will you."

"Come on, Tommy, you know I been waiting for this. We been talking about this for weeks. I know you started setting it up. I heard you talking to the guys."

Since he was awake now, Ilford fluffed up the pillows and sat up in bed. "Yeah, I hear about it every day," he said, taking a cigarette out of the package next to the bed, lighting it and blowing the smoke up to the ceiling.

"It makes me excited, Honey, just thinking about it."

"I don't think I can stand any more excitement just now," he said.

"Come on, Tommy, excitement is what it's all about," she whispered in his ear. "I keep things interesting, and there's nothing I wouldn't do for you. You know that."

"Yeah, yeah, yeah."

"Come on, Baby, you like the excitement. It wouldn't do, would it, for a big, bad gangster like you to have some soccer mom for your bitch? You know, some middle-aged drone driving a mini-van."

"Not much danger 'a that," he said.

"Never can tell," she said.

"I ain't seen many soccer bitches at the dogfights, Roxellana."

"Maybe you just haven't looked right, Tommy. They're probably there stalking you."

"I don't think so," he snorted.

"I might stalk you," she giggled in his ear.

He hit her with a pillow and said, "That's what I do to stalkers."

She laughed and said, "Come on Tommy, when is the dogfight?."

"What do you like so well about this dogfight, little bitch?" he said.

"I don't know, Sweetie, I think I just want to see what it's like for a dog to kill a man. I want to watch him die," she cooed as she stretched her back with her arms high over her head.

"Yeah, you're just like them high rollers who are gonna buy tickets to this thing. They like that too."

"Don't you like it, Honey?" she cooed.

"Hell no, I don't like it," he said, recoiling a little. "Why do I want to watch some derelict get mauled by dogs? You're a sick little number," he said.

"Then why do you do it?" she said.

"That's a damned good question. I wonder that myself sometimes. If you hadn't pushed it, I wouldn't be doin it."

"Even if the money...," she paused.

"Yeah, well, there's some money in it," he said.

"Tommy, you're so sweet to me. But I really want to see it. When's it gonna be?"

"Well," he said, "we got to have a trial run first. We got to kill a few derelicts to see how it goes, how the dogs do it, how long it takes them. We got to time them so we know how to rig the bets."

"Yeah I know, but we been planning this forever. When are you finally gonna let the dogs kill someone?"

Ilford looked a the ceiling as if he had not heard her. She looked at him to see why he wasn't answering, Then he said, "Tomorrow."

"Tomorrow?" Roxellana sat up in bed. "Tomorrow?" she squealed.

"Yeah," Ilford growled, happy that he had made her happy.

"Oh, Tommy. That's great. I'm so excited. I'm not letting you out of my sight until we get there. I don't want you going without me."

"Don't worry, Sweet Stuff, you'll be right there with me."

"You're actually going to let the dogs kill somebody?" she said, excitedly.

"Wouldn't be much point in doin it without killin 'em would it? I mean, we're doin' this to see how long it takes to ice 'em. If I don't know that, I'll lose money when the high rollers start betting on the real thing. I got to know how long it takes. That's what this is all about, Honey," he said.

"I know, Tommy. I'm so excited."

Chapter 11

But that was the week before.

The week after the dog fight, Ilford stormed up and down his office, fuming and gesticulating, his neck swollen with rage, while a group of twenty employees sat and stood, silent and fearful, as he shouted and blustered himself red in the face.

"Nobody," and here Ilford paused, spittle dribbling down his lips, "Nobody puts the finger on Tom Ilford. Nobody. You hear?" he bellowed. His face was distorted by anger.

The men said nothing as he resumed pacing back and forth, yelling, outraged, making a fist, punching the air, pounding on the desk, and coming very near to busting both bulging veins out of his beet-red forehead. When the tirade stopped, he stared at them, exhausted, panting. They were silent, apprehensive. No one spoke.

"Now listen to me you sonsofbitches. One of you did this. I don't know who. But I'll find out. You think you can photograph me watching some derelict get torn up by dogs and then extort money for the film. It ain't gonna happen. Whoever you are, you'll be dead," he snarled. "I promise you. You'll be dead. Now get the fuck out of here."

Silently, the men moved toward the door, anxious to escape. "Skeeter," Ilford growled, "you stay."

A forty year old man with a pear shaped body turned and looked at Ilford. Disappointment and fear registered on his face. He was hoping he could get the hell out of there with everyone else, but escape was not for him.

"Sit down, Skeeter," Ilford said, his face in his hands, bags under his eyes.

Skeeter took a seat in front of Ilford's desk. He wore a wrinkled gray pinstripe suit and a shirt that had formerly been white, but now simply formed a yellowish backdrop for the cheap polka dot tie that dangled loose around his neck.

The room was virtually empty now and the last man out was closing the door. Ilford slouched in his chair.

Skeeter was an investigator in the DA's office when Ilford first met him fifteen years ago. The DA was on the take, and when the DA failed to prosecute a prominent mobster in a murder case, who had paid the DA to avoid the prosecution, the newspapers got hold of information that there had been a payoff. The only way the DA could extricate himself was to have a fall-guy. That's where Skeeter came in. Skeeter agreed to say that he had lost or contaminated critical evidence and that's why the prosecution could not be continued. Of course, Skeeter lost his job, and Tommy Ilford, a sometime acquaintance of the DA, took Skeeter on his payroll as a favor. That had been eight years ago. Now Skeeter was a trusted employee.

"I want you to find out who sent this," Ilford said.

"I'll do what I can," Skeeter ventured uncertainly.

"What the hell does that mean. You're the investigator, aren't you? I want you to find out who wrote this letter, get all the tapes, and kill him. That's not too difficult, is it?" Ilford spat.

"I dunno boss. It's been a long time since I was an investigator. But if I was to try to remember how to do this shit, you just start with simple stuff. You start with the facts, the simple facts. So, what we got is you kill some guy in a dog fight and now some prick puts the squeeze on you to pay a hundred grand. The first question might be how does some guy get in the barn to take pictures, and how does he even know you're gonna be there?"

"Yeah. So... And what's the answer to them questions?"

"There must'a been thirty people at that dogfight, all of 'em working for us. Maybe I'll start by figuring out who was there and who was not."

"Yeah, and see if any of 'em fool with cameras."

"Okay, Boss, I'll make a list of who was there, the dog handlers, the drivers, the grounds people, the building guards, the girlfriends — I saw girlfriends there — and I'll interview them."

"Damn right you'll interview them. You find out who the hell it was. Somebody made this tape," pounding his fist on a VHS cassette on his desk.

"All right, boss. I'm on it. Anything else?"

"Hell yes, there's something else. Have you forgotten that two of the derelicts we kidnapped to use as bait in the dogfights got away? They're as much a threat as this fuckin tape. While you're working on who sent this tape, have Claude and Mel look for the derelicts. They live around here. It shouldn't be too hard to find them. But it has to be fast, before they have a chance to start blabbing."

"Okay"

"You understand, don't you, that if it gets out that we had these dogfights to kill derelicts, I'm gonna be prosecuted for murder.?"

"Yeah, boss, I figured that."

"Well, what you may not have figured is that you're all gonna be prosecuted if I am. We were all in this together, and if I swing, you and everyone else will too. You got it?"

"Yes sir."

"Then get the fuck out of here," Ilford said, "And tell the others what I said. Maybe that will light a fire under your asses."

Chapter 12

After Roxellana left, Eric went downhill. He began to spend more time in the bars. He stashed a bottle or two at home. He would fuck any girl who would have him, and he generally drifted from one thing to another without much thought. He could not get over her. She had, he told himself, ruined his life. He had no friends. Even Celeste was gone. He was a drunk. He had no place to go other than where he was. And his boss was fucking his girl.

But now, after six months, Roxellana had invited him to meet her at lunch in the student union. He had avoided thinking about what he had become during that time. As he sat there waiting, however, it was difficult to avoid the conclusion that he was pathetic. She calls and I come, he thought. She walks out on me, moves in with my boss, and then tells me to meet her for lunch. And I do it. Maybe Ilford treats her bad. That's why she wants to see me, he thought. She wants to tell me all about it. When he saw her come in the door, he swallowed hard. She looked even better than he remembered. She saw him and walked up to the table.

"How ya been?" He tried to appear cool, smooth, a little disinterested even, but as soon as he did it, he knew she could see through his pretenses.

"I been great, Eric, and I'm so glad to see you." She gave him a hug and a big kiss. "Come on. Let's get some lunch."

They went through the cafeteria line, got their trays, and sat at a table apart from the main lunch crowd.

"So why did you call me?" Eric said, chewing his hamburger. "You decide you want to move back in to the doghouse?"

"No, but I got a business deal for you. Maybe a way for you to move out of the doghouse yourself."

Eric had difficulty concealing his disappointment. She wasn't going to complain about Ilford after all. "The doghouse ain't too bad," he said, quietly.

"Get real," she said.

"I am real," he said, a little petulantly. "It may not be good enough for you, but I like it fine."

"Look, Eric, it was an opportunity for me, and I took it."

"Yeah, I can see that."

"Well, you and I don't have to be strangers," she teased over her sandwich.

"Oh? Yeah. We'd both end up dead."

"I don't think so."

"You mean you got Ilford so tied up he'd even let you screw your old boyfriend?"

"Probably," she said, taking a large bite out of her sandwich.

"Is that what you want to do?" he asked.

"Not right now," she said with her mouth full. "Maybe later. I told you. I got a business deal for you."

"What is it?"

"You remember how I needed money?"

"Yeah," he said.

"Well, I got a way to get some money. Big money."

"What do you want money for now? Ilford will probably give you whatever you want," he said, with a tinge of resentment in his voice.

"First of all, that's not true. Second, it's none of your damned business," she said, selecting a potato chip and snapping it in two with her teeth, "and third, I need my own money."

"Okay. Okay," he said. "But I'm not gonna stand between you and any more pissed-off boyfriends."

"You don't have to," she said. "All you have to do is run a camera at a dogfight."

"Why would I wanna do that?"

"To collect fifty grand."

"First of all, Mr. Ilford don't allow cameras at the dogfights, and secondly, how could running a camera be worth fifty grand?"

"Did you know that Ilford's mixed up with the mob in Las Vegas?"

"Yeah? So what?"

"Some of the mob's customers are really high rollers and they like to bet on weird shit. Big money. I've convinced Tommy..."

"Tommy?"

"Yeah, Ilford. I've convinced Ilford that he can make really big money by running a special kind of dogfight."

"What's so special about a dogfight?"

"Most dogfights don't end up killing people?"

"Killing people?"

"Yeah. The idea is that you put people — derelicts probably — in the fighting ring and turn the dogs loose. You time how long it takes the dogs to kill the person and the audience bets on how long it will take."

"Jesus, Roxellana. You must be nuts."

"No, Eric, it will work. Tommy's already put some feelers out in Vegas and they want to come."

"Yeah, it might work. But killing somebody so that people can bet money is nuts."

"It's not nuts, Eric. It's business."

"Well, I won't have anything to do with it."

"You haven't even heard your part yet."

"I don't care what you think my part is, I won't do it."

"Just listen. It's not bad. All you have to do is secretly photograph the trial runs."

"What trial runs?"

"Well, in order for Tommy — Ilford — to make money, he has to know how long it is going to take the dogs to kill the derelicts. So he needs to set up a trial fight where the dogs go after a few of them and we time how long it takes."

"And I'm supposed to stand there photographing this? Ilford's not gonna go for that."

"Ilford's not gonna know, Eric. That's the whole idea. At the trial fights there will only be a few people. You're going to tape a camera up high somewhere in the barn where it can't be seen. And you're going to turn it on when the fights start. I know you can do that because you showed me how you could start a video camera by remote control."

"Supposing I did this. How does that turn out to be worth fifty grand?"

"You're going to send the tape to Tommy — Ilford — with a demand for a hundred grand, fifty for you and fifty for me, or we turn the tape over to the newspapers."

Eric bolted up from the table, his half eaten sandwich dangling from one hand. He stared at Roxellana in utter disbelief, unable to speak.

"Sit down, Honey," Roxellana cooed. "I won't let Tommy hurt you. You'll be fine and we'll both have lots of money. Hell, Tommy won't even miss it."

Eric sat down and put his sandwich down. "Roxellana," he finally said, "That's suicide. I won't do it. I'm not gonna have any part of this and if you're smart, you won't either."

"There's no doubt you're gonna do this, Baby," Roxellana said.

"You're totally out of your mind," he said. "I'm not doin anything."

"If you don't, I will go to Tommy and tell him you called me and asked me out to lunch and tried to get me to go along with this idea of yours," she said.

"He'd never believe you," he stammered. "I didn't even know about this dog and man fight until you told me. How could I think up something I didn't even know about?"

"I'd just tell him that I told you about it earlier. We're still friends, and I let it slip when we were talking on the phone that we were gonna have a dogfight where people get killed. You're one of his dog handlers, after all. You'd know sooner or later, so the slip wouldn't be so bad. And then after I told you, you thought about it for a while and then came up with this idea to make money."

"You think he would believe that?"

"I know he'd believe it, Eric. He believes whatever I tell him."

Chapter 13

In the early evening of the day he had met with Roxellana, Eric drove his old Tacoma pickup truck to the south side, where Celeste hung out. After an hour of going in an out of depressing coffeehouses that seemed to be trying to imitate San Francisco of the 1950's, Eric found her huddled in a corner, staring at the wall. Celeste had gone here even when she lived with him, and Eric figured he'd find her near her old haunts.

"Celeste, It's me, Eric," he said.

She looked at him in a daze.

"Eric?"

"Yeah. Come on, Celeste. I'm taking you home."

"Home? I don't live with you, Eric. I'm not going anywhere with you."

"Let's go, Celeste. I need you to go with me," he pleaded.

"Fuck you, Eric," she said, her eyes glassed over a bit.

"Have you been back on the smack?"

"I had a little earlier on. What do you want?"

"I want you to come home with me. I need to talk to you."

"Have a cup of coffee," she smiled hazily, "and I'll consider it. I consider all offers," she snickered.

Eric had coffee and got a large coffee for Celeste. An hour later, she agreed to go home with him. "But just so you remember," she said, "I don't live with you."

"I know. But tonight you do. Come on."

Eric took Celeste to the East Liberty doghouse and tucked her in. There would be time to talk in the morning. There was plenty to talk about. He needed help. He needed an ally, a friend. He needed someone to help him sort this out.

In the morning, Eric climbed into bed with Celeste and the two made love. Both had been abandoned and they were both hungry for companionship. They clung together.

At breakfast, Eric said, "Celeste, I need to talk to you."

"Go ahead," she smiled. She was beginning to warm up to the idea of a homecoming.

"I know you don't want to hear this, but Roxellana has me in a jam. She wants me to help her screw the boss."

"I can't believe she needs your help," she laughed.

"No. I'm serious. She wants me to help her threaten to expose him unless he pays us — her and me — a hundred thousand dollars."

"A hundred thousand dollars? What do you mean, expose him?"

"She's talked him into having some dogfights where men get put in the fighting ring and the dogs kill them."

"Holy shit, Eric," she said, her eyes popping wide. "That's the craziest thing I ever heard. Why would anyone want to kill people in a dog ring? "

"Because some high rollers from Vegas want to bet on how long it takes the dogs to kill a man."

"That's sick."

"I know. That's what I told her."

"And she wants you to handle the dogs?"

"That's not all. She wants me to rig up a hidden video camera in the barn and film the dogfights, then threaten Ilford with the film unless he pays us a hundred thousand dollars."

"He'll kill you."

"I know. I told her that too."

"Jesus. What are you going to do? You can't do this."

"If I don't do it she says she'll go to Ilford and tell him that I came to her with this idea. She would be exposing me to him as the guy who wants to frame him with murder and extort money at the same time."

"Oh, Eric. This bitch is evil. I knew she wasn't right, but I had no idea she could come up with something like this. I couldn't figure out why you didn't see how weird she was."

"Yeah, well, you're right. I should have known after she told me about her father."

"What about him," Celeste said, curling her feet under her and sipping coffee.

"Her father wouldn't let her do what she wanted or give her the money she wanted, so she got him drunk and seduced him and filmed the whole thing."

"Jesus Christ," Celeste said, "Why? How would that help her?"

"She threatened to turn over the film to the bank where he worked if he didn't give her what she wanted. Money and a car."

"That's it? Money and a car? The bitch fucked her own father for money and a car?"

"Yeah."

"You're right. She's worse than I thought. In fact, she's unbelievable," Celeste said.

"I just don't know what to do. If I run away, she'll tell him I came up with this idea and he'll hunt me down and kill me: and if I don't run away, I have to do what she says."

"I think she's got you boxed in," Celeste said.

"Yeah."

"Jesus, Eric."

Chapter 14

The big GMC pickup sped along back roads headed out of the city through the early hours of the morning. Two men in the cab. Three men in the bed. The men in the bed lay in a heap and didn't move. Their heads bumped against the flooring and their bodies rolled together in a lump when the truck rounded a corner. One of the men, John Derringer, the one with the pony tail, had put away the best part of a quart of whiskey over the course of the evening, washed down with two quarts of beer. His friends, Zorba and Arnie, were pikers by comparison, but they too had drunk enough to send ordinary people into cardiac arrest. The men in the cab were tough guys, muscle men, steroid heads, who worked for Ilford. They had Shanghaied the men in the back and were headed for a barn north of Pittsburgh.

John Derringer was about five-ten, a hundred and sixty pounds, sinewy. His hair was tied back in a pony tail. His arms were strong, but not big. Ropes of muscle wrapped around bones. The ropes of muscle were attached to oversized wrists, and the wrists, in turn were attached to very large hands. The men John worked with called them "cement hands." When John hit someone with one of the big hands it was like getting hit with a concrete block.

Derringer's face was old beyond his years, probably from decades of hard drinking. He was in his mid-forties, but his face looked like he was seventy. It was full of deep creases that ran through the weathered skin. Two of Derringer's front teeth were missing and he wore his hair in a pony tail held in place by a bandanna. He looked like Willie Nelson on hard times, but with more creases.

Occasionally Derringer's eyes would open and he would see the night sky blurring past him in a rush. Then they would round a corner and bump over something, and he would collide with the insensible bodies of his buddies. They would roll over on him and obscure his vision, and he would slip back into a troubled stupor.

On this particular evening, John had followed his current favorite squeeze to the Cutfahrt Bar in the West End of Pittsburgh. John's buddies Zorba and Arnie were there too, and all were pretty well lubricated by 1:00 a.m. John had even forgotten about the pain in his back and the squeeze was nowhere to be seen. He had spent the day on a roof, working as a day laborer, and his back was killing him. The effects of the handful of aspirin he had taken earlier in the day had worn off long ago, and he sought relief in the bottle.

A little after one fifteen, two young men dressed in jeans and windbreakers came into the bar. They seemed to study the occupants of the bar for a time, and then they approached John's table.

"You boys like a little more to drink?" one of the men said to the table at large.

"What you got?" Zorba said.

"What you want?" the man said.

"How about a bottle of Jack Daniels?" Arnie ventured.

"No problem," the man said. His partner went to the bar and bought a bottle, then brought it to the table.

"Damn," Zorba slurred, pouring drinks all around from the new bottle. The men sat at the table, but didn't drink.

By 2:00 a.m. the three Jack Daniels drinkers were nearly passed out, and the two men who were sitting with them helped them out to their truck, where they piled them into the bed and drove off.

A full moon was out and clouds whipped across the bright September sky. The men in the cab were glad they had worn their jackets. The men in the bed of the truck had no idea that they were cold.

* * *

While some people drink to chase their demons away, John Derringer drank to dull the pain. He had broken his back as a child by falling out of a tree. They told him he'd never walk again. But he was determined to prove them wrong. He spent a year in various casts, and at the end of the year, he was so weak that he could barely lift his arm. But he was determined. When he told them he would walk, they tried to discourage his fantasies. Then he began lifting things. First a can of soup, then a telephone book, then a four pound weight. Then weights in both hands. Then heavier weights. Then he demanded to be given crutches and then to be put on the rails where he would support himself with his arms and try to move his lifeless legs. After two years of daily struggle, one leg moved slightly, then the other. Six months later, the legs could support his body and a year after that he was walking. Now, an adult, he walked, albeit with a limp and a bit of pain, but he walked.

John was never interested in formal schooling and because he was out of school so much, he studied at home. When he turned thirteen, he passed the GED test and got a high school diploma. After that, he read books on mechanics, engineering and boat building. By the time he was twenty, he had apprenticed as a plumber, an electrician, an auto mechanic, a welder, a diesel mechanic, a marine technician and a heating and air conditioning man. The consensus was that if it was broke, John could fix it.

But he couldn't fix the pain. It was always with him and when it was bad, he drank to get past it. When he was in the midst of a job and the pain started, he would take a handful of aspirin, fifteen to twenty at a time, to keep going, but at night when there was no work to distract him, the aspirin didn't work and he turned to the booze. The drinking sometimes turned into binges, and when that happened, the various jobs went the way of all things mortal. "He's the best man I ever had on the job," one foreman said, "but I need him to be here. I can't hold his job open for two weeks while he gets through being drunk."

The barkeep at the Cutfahrt Bar used to say that John was one-half genius, one-half irresponsible drunk, one-half pussywhipped by his barfly girlfriends, and one-half the meanest sonofabitch he ever heard of. When John pointed out that if the barkeep was right, there must be two of him, the barkeep vowed to kill himself on the spot if another John Derringer showed up. John just grinned his crooked grin.

When John woke up, it was midmorning and he was lying in the bed of a pickup truck parked in a field next to a huge barn. He pulled himself upright, squinting out the sun, and he could see nothing but a distant tree line. But as he sat there, he realized his hands were duct taped behind him and he saw that Zorba and Arnie were bound with tape also. They were still asleep.

As he looked around and tried to figure out where he was and what was happening, a caravan of cars and trucks appeared coming through the treeline, three hundred yards distant. Gradually as they approached, he could see the caravan consisted of a luxury sedan followed by several pickup trucks and two SUVs. The luxury sedan stopped next to the truck he was in. One of the young men from last night got out of the cab of the truck when the cars pulled up and greeted the man who got out of the car.

The man was tall, middle-aged, strong, but a little out of shape, wearing khakis, and a brightly colored sweater and sunglasses.

"You get the bums?" he said to the young man.

"Yes sir, they're in the back here," the young man said, pointing to the bed of his truck and Dillinger.

"Any trouble?"

"No, sir. They came quietly. They were all drunked up."

"Do they know anything?"

"No, sir. Didn't talk to them hardly at all. Just got them a bottle and they fucked themselves up for us."

It was plain to Derringer that playing the outraged citizen would be one of the more pointless acts he could imagine, so he just watched and listened. Zorba and Arnie were still dead to the world.

"We'll get the dogs in place and you bring them in, one at a time, when we're ready. I'll let you know," the boss man said.

The boss man and two bodyguard types got back in the car and drove another 200 yards to the barn. Two of the pickup trucks pulled up near the door of the barn and several men lifted down cages containing dogs. On the ground, they opened the cages and put leashes on three large Pit Bulls. They led them into the barn. Other young men and some girls got out of the other vehicles and went into the barn also.

Ten minutes later, a man came out of the barn and walked up to the pickup truck where John and his two buddies were tied up.

"They're ready," he said.

"All right," the driver said. "Help me get one of them out of the truck."

The two men came around to the back of the truck and unhooked the tailgate. Derringer didn't like the way things were shaping up. Tied up, remote location, big-ass dogs, fancy dancy pissant with bodyguards, taking them in one at a time. His stomach tightened and his mind raced with possibilities.

The two men pulled a semi-conscious Arnie out of the back of the truck, cut the tape on his hands, and half-walked, half-carried him into the barn. When they were out of hearing, Derringer began to work on ripping the tape on his hands against sharp edges of the truck. No good. He scooted over to Zorba's semi-conscious body and, his hand behind his back, patted Zorba's front pockets for a pocket knife. He found one and painfully extracted it from Zorba's pocket, then got it open and began sawing the tape on his wrists.

As he broke his arms free from the tape, he began to hear growling and then almost immediately, screaming from the barn. It was Arnie. It sounded as if the dogs had been set on him. Damn. There were growling and tearing sounds, and then suddenly, Arnie's screaming stopped. The growling reached a crescendo and simultaneously there was the sound of "Ohhhhhhhhhh," from the spectators. Then silence. The whole thing had taken less than three minutes. Zorba was beginning to stir now. Derringer crawled over and cut the tape on his wrists.

"Listen to me and get it fuckin right the first time," Derringer hissed into Zorba's ear. "Some dudes have kidnapped us. We're in a truck. They took Arnie in that barn and I think they killed him. That's what they're gonna do to us."

Zorba's eyes opened and he stared at Derringer.

"No shit?"

"No shit, brother. I'm cutting your hands loose. They'll be comin' out for us in a minute, so just keep your hands behind your back like you're tied up and wait for my move," Derringer said.

"Okay" Zorba said, blinking in the sun, trying to wake up.

"Get on the other side of the truck next to the tailgate. Put your feet up against mine. Get your head clear. We're gonna have to take these bastards out."

"I'm ready," Zorba said, trying to convince himself he was awake.

Chapter 15

Celeste had tears in her eyes as she sat in the cab of Eric's Toyota pickup, the three big cages of the dogs in the bed clattering and banging when the truck went over bumps in the dirt road.

"I need you here, Celeste," he said. "I can't do this myself. I need somebody to help me. I'm so confused I don't know what to do. If you don't help me with this, I'll screw it up, and then she'll tell Ilford I thought it up and he'll kill me."

"I know, Eric, but I don't want to even think about this. Do you realize you're asking me to watch these dogs rip a man apart and kill him? I can't even imagine it."

"Just stick with me, Celeste. I know it's hard, but I don't have anywhere else to turn, and I need you there to start that camera because no matter what she thinks, I can't. I'll be busy with the dogs."

"Did you set up the camera?"

"Yeah, I went out yesterday. I pretended I needed to make sure the fight ring was okay for the dogs. They left me alone and I taped the camera in a place where nobody can see it, but it covers the ring."

"Did you bring the remote starter?"

"Yeah, I got it."

"Damn, Eric. I'm scared. I don't want to do this. I don't want to be here."

"You've got to do it for me, Celeste. All you have to do is push the button and it will start. Whenever they bring in another guy, just push the button and film it. Just sit there. You don't have to watch."

Eric followed the truck in front of him through the trees. Once out of the trees and into a field, a large barn with vertical wood siding was visible three hundred yards from the trees. Eric maneuvered the truck slowly over the dirt road to the barn, trying to be gentle with the dogs. He stopped near the open door of the barn and got out of the truck. Two other handlers helped him offload the dogs, still in their cages and snarling. They knew that they were near the dog ring and they anticipated action.

Celeste went into the stands where the audience would sit in a real dogfight and sat, hunched up in her coat. Two dozen other people milled around. Ilford finally came in the barn and, with the pink-pants-suited Roxellana parading in his wake, the two sat in the box seats right on the edge of the ring. Various hangers-on came and paid their respects to Ilford. Roxellana sat there like a queen, basking in the glory of being Ilford's girlfriend.

Within ten minutes, Ilford ordered the dogs out of their cages and three handlers held them on leashes at three different points of the ring. The dogs strained and turned in circles, dancing and twirling on their leashes, trying to get loose and start the action, whatever it was, snarling and snapping at anything that moved.

Finally, two of Ilford's men arrived with Arnie. One on each side, they propped him up, keeping him upright. When they got to the edge of the fight ring, Arnie dug his heels in and said, "No, I ain't going in there."

Celeste pressed the button and stole a glance toward the hidden camera. She could see the red light glowing now. It was on.

"You goin, my man," the big one said, and punched him in the side of the head.

Arnie went slack and the two big men dragged him over the edge of the fight ring and dropped him in the middle. The dogs strained and yelped all around him. The two big men backed out of the ring. Arnie lay there for a minute, stunned, and then got up on all fours.

"Loose," Ilford said.

At once, the three dogs leapt into the ring and two actually collided with each other in their frenzy to get their teeth into Arnie. Arnie made an effort to get to his feet, but he never made it. The first dog hit him from behind between the shoulders and sent him sprawling into the dirt. The two dogs who had collided recovered quickly and got to their feet. One dug into Arnie's foot and the other attacked his head. The first dog had him by the arm and sometimes by the shoulder.

Arnie's body was dragged back and forth across the ring, sometimes by his head, sometimes by his feet, sometimes sideways by his shoulder. Through it all, he screamed, "Get them off. Get them off. Get them off. They're killing me. Somebody, help."

According to the official timekeeper, Arnie lost all signs of resistance at one minute, forty-seven seconds. That was recorded as the time it took to kill him. And in fact, he was dead.

The handlers seemed to be dazed by what they had witnessed and stood watching as the dogs tore at Arnie's remains. Finally, Ilford yelled at them and they went into the ring with leashes to pull the dogs off. They struggled to snap the leashes onto the snarling, moving dogs, who were busy biting and ripping the inert body. Even after the handlers had the leashes snapped onto the massive leather collars of each dog, the dogs strained to get back to the carcass, which was covered with blood and ripped clothing. One of Arnie's femurs stuck jaggedly through what was left of his pants legs.

It took all six men to get the dogs back into their cages. Even then, the dogs continued growling and snapping their teeth for four or five minutes after the last cage door was slammed shut.

The same two men who had forced Arnie to his death now dragged the torn, dead body out of the barn.

"Bring in the next one," Ilford said.

Celeste could not hear what they said, but Roxellana was hanging on Ilford's shoulder and whispering excitedly in his ear. Time seemed to slog on forever, and periodically Celeste snuck glances at the hidden camera. She pushed the remote button and the light went off. She would wait until the next victim arrived to activate the camera again.

Time continued to pass endlessly and nothing was happening. The dogs were still in their cages and the men had not come back with another victim. Celeste saw Ilford motion to one of his men and then the man went out of the barn toward the truck where the victims were being held.

Within two minutes, he was back, running, breathless, talking excitedly to Ilford. Ilford then began shouting and all the men ran out of the barn toward the truck.

Celeste, hesitantly, went down to where Roxellana was sitting.

"What happened?" she said.

Roxellana surveyed her coolly, and said, "Apparently the other derelicts got away."

"How could that be?"

"I have no idea," Roxellana said. I hope you did your job. Eric told me why you're here."

"I did it," Celeste whispered, almost to herself.

"Good. Now keep your mouth shut and do what Eric tells you. Otherwise you're both dead," Roxellana hissed.

Chapter 16

Derringer got himself and Zorba into sitting positions, hands behind their backs, on opposite sides of the tailgate. It wasn't too much of a stretch for Zorba to feign a drunken stupor. Now and then Derringer would whisper directions as he thought of something. As he spoke, the two could hear Arnie's cries for help and the ungodly growling of the dogs and tearing sounds as every inch of Arnie's clothing was shredded.

Between Arnie's screams and Derringer's kicking him in the legs, Zorba gradually woke up, and he even managed to repeat Derringer's directions about what they were going to do. The screams stopped, then the growling and snarling and ripping sounds stopped, and everything was quiet. Zorba and Derringer sat sweating in the late morning sun, waiting uneasily. Finally, two heavies came out of the barn, dragging Arnie by his heels. As they got closer, Derringer could see that Arnie's body was a ripped mass of red meat and his face was unrecognizable. They dropped Arnie's lifeless legs when they reached the side of the truck and looked at Derringer and Zorba as if they expected them to say something. Neither spoke. The men came around to the end of the truck and released the tailgate.

Just as Derringer had told him to do, Zorba started scooting away from the tailgate, as did Derringer, but Derringer lagged a little behind. The bigger of the two men leaned into the bed of the truck to grab Derringer's leg and Derringer kicked him hard on the tip of his chin. It was a perfectly placed kick, not too hard, at the sweet spot that always spells knockout. The big man's upper body collapsed on the bed of the truck.

The second man clambered into the truck bed, not to be intimidated by drunken derelicts, and the instant his weight was equally distributed on all fours, Derringer's cement fist hit him just below the ear. As he dropped, Derringer, who was more or less lying down, spun around on his butt and kicked the man in the head, knocking him out of the truck and onto the ground, where he lay in an unconscious heap.

"Help me pull this one into the truck," Derringer said to Zorba, pointing to the man who was half in and half out of the truck bed.

Zorba scooted out the back of the truck and lifted the big man's legs while Derringer tugged his shoulders into the bed of the truck. Zorba closed the tailgate and ran around to the cab. Derringer pulled the keys from the big man's pockets, vaulted over the side of the truck and jumped into the cab.

The V8 engine rumbled to life when Derringer turned the key, and he jammed the gear lever into Drive. The truck spun out a little at first until the traction system kicked in and then it sped past the other vehicles still parked in the field. Derringer was on the throttle and the truck bumped like crazy, heading toward the tree line where Derringer had seen the cars enter the field. As they approached the trees, the road became clear and they disappeared into the foilage. The tree line was only thirty yards deep, however, and on the other side of the woods, they could see the dirt road they were on winding up a slight grade to a blacktop road. Derringer stayed on the throttle, crashing the big truck through the gate at the edge of the field, then squealing and sliding sideways onto the blacktop.

"Shit, I know where we are," Zorba said, now wide awake. "My mom grew up around here. We're in Bell Township, you know, not far from Apollo."

"Am I going the right way?" Derringer said.

"Yeah, turn left. We're headed toward Apollo, but they'll be on us when they find out we're gone," Zorba said. "Turn again on that gravel road."

Derringer wheeled the big truck to the left down a narrow road with a sign that said "Pavement Ends." Half a mile down the road, the pavement did end and the truck was in a thick veil of trees on a gravel and mud road that was not often traveled. They had to slow to climb over fallen limbs and exposed rocks the size of basketballs.

"Is our friend still in the back?" Derringer said, concentrating on the road.

Zorba twisted in the seat. "He's still there."

Derringer drove on for another fifteen minutes and then stopped the truck in a grove of trees.

"Let's talk to our boy," Derringer said. He pulled the keys from the ignition and pocketed them. Both men got out of the cab. Zorba grabbed a hammer that was on the floor. The heavy in the back was just coming around and trying to sit up, shaking his head, as if to shake the fuzziness out of his eyes.

Derringer lowered the tailgate and the two escapees pulled the gangster toward them by grabbing his ankles.

He was still too groggy to resist. They pulled him out of the truck and allowed him to fall on the ground. With the big man on his back and Zorba straddling his head with the hammer poised, Derringer went through the man's pockets. He extracted a pocket knife, change, a cell phone and a wallet. The man's driver's license identified him as Harvey Larrimore. Derringer pocketed the driver's license.

The big man watched Derringer, his eyes looking for an opportunity to resist, but he could see the hammer in Zorba's hand and he knew he was too groggy to be sure of himself, so he just lay there.

"I guess you were gonna kill us?" Derringer asked.

The man said nothing.

Derringer had the man's folded pocket knife concealed in his right hand. The end of the handle protruded two inches from the heel of his hand. He brought the pommel of the knife down on the man's left knee with a powerful backhand. The big man let out a bellowing roar of pain and involuntarily sat up, reaching for his knee. As he came up, Derringer hit him with a right cross to the mouth with the pommel of the knife, knocking him back down on his back.

The man lay there moaning, bleeding from his mouth, reaching feebly for his knee, which now wouldn't bend.

"All right Harvey," Derringer said. "It don't look to me like you're very good at pain. Now, you answer my questions or I'll bust you up so you'll never walk again, and believe me, I know how to do it."

"All right," the big man said.

"Why did you kidnap us and why did you kill my friend?" Derringer said.

"Look man, I didn't kill nobody. I just work for the man and he said to go get three derelicts for the dogs. That's all."

"What do you mean, for the dogs?"

"Oh, Christ, you aren't gonna kill me, are you?"

"Just talk or you wont be able to talk," Derringer growled.

"The man, he's got these Pit Bulls, and he fights them, and he's selling tickets to a fight where the dogs kill a man."

"There weren't many people there," Derringer said.

"No, this wasn't the fight. It was just a practice to see how long it would take the dogs to kill a man."

"Jesus Christ," Zorba said.

"And you went along with this?" Derringer said.

"I didn't have no choice, man. Once you work for them, you do what they say or you're dead."

"Who was the man in the fancy car?"

"That was the boss. His name is Tom Ilford."

"You mean the big drug dealer?"

"Yeah. That's him."

"What do you do for him?"

"Whatever he tells me."

"Why is he involved in this dog thing?"

"There's a lot of money to be made in dog fighting. It's mostly in the betting. But now that he's got this new idea ..."

"You mean having the dogs kill people?"

"Yeah. Now that he's doing that, there's going to be a lot more money in dog fighting."

"How much does it cost to go to one of these dogfights?" Derringer said.

"He's charging two thousand dollars a seat for this one that's coming up."

"Who goes?"

"It's all big wigs, man. All big wigs."

"All right, Harvey," Derringer said. "We're gonna leave you here. I'm letting you live, but if you tell them anything about us, I'll come back and find you. You just tell them you were knocked out and we dumped you off and you didn't see nothing."

"Okay. I didn't see nothing," he repeated, cradling his knee in both hands and rocking back and forth, "But I'll give you some advice. Get out of town and don't stop running. He'll find you. And he might find you even if you run. He's gonna be pissed."

"I'll give *you* some advice, Harvey. Get another job."

Derringer pocketed Harvey's knife and his cell phone and got back in the truck.

"Are they gonna kill us, John?" Zorba said.

"They gonna try," Derringer said.

Chapter 17

Sam and Nick sat on one side of the booth in the Sunrise Café. Detective Frank Stone sat on the other side. Everyone was having eggs and bacon, potatoes and coffee.

"So why'd they pull you off the Inverlok thing, Frank?" Sam asked.

"Pass the ketchup, will you? I got no clue," taking the ketchup from Nick. "Things was goin along like they always do and I thought I was getting somewhere and all of a sudden, I get a call to put it on the back burner," he said. "Then you guys call me and tell me you're interested in who done it."

Frank Stone, Sam and Nick met a year earlier when Sam and Nick were hired to protect a woman who was being stalked by a local rich boy who raped her and then decided to kill her. When Stone tried to pursue the investigation of the rich-guy-rapist, he was called off by his superiors. The fix was in. Money buys fixes. But it didn't buy Stone, and he teamed up with Sam and Nick, in a quiet way, to flush out the rich guy. The same thing was happening now.

"You got a file we can look at?" Nick said.

"Sure. I brought it along," Stone said.

"Got anything in particular that interested you?" Sam asked.

"Well, two things really," Stone said with his mouth full, waving a piece of toast. "First, the dead guy comes from a rich family. Second, one of the things I found in his desk was a tape of him fucking some girl."

"Not his wife?" Nick said.

"Not his wife," Stone said.

"Why do you think you were pulled off?" Sam said.

"Can't figure it out," Stone said. "He comes from a rich family. You'd think the money would buy a full squadron of detectives."

"Maybe there's something more important than money," Sam suggested.

"Gimmie a break, Sam. We're talking about cops here. There's nothing more important than money," Stone said.

"Okay, then, how about a long-term relationship that — in the long run — makes more money," Sam said.

"Like what?"

"I don't know. Like maybe Scuilli, the D.A., or some mobster that sends in a bag of cash every week. Maybe the mobster killed the guy and he doesn't want to get convicted," Sam said.

"A college professor?"

"I know. Why would they kill a college professor?" Sam said.

"Yeah," Stone chewed.

"Drugs?" Nick said.

"The guy's clean," Stone said.

"Did you interview this girl?" Sam said.

"Yeah. I had a hell of a time finding her. She left her apartment some time ago and apparently started shacking up with some kid. But when I finally found the kid over in a run-down part of East Liberty, she wasn't there. I finally found her in an apartment of her own in Shadyside."

"How did Inverlok meet her? Is she a student?" Nick said.

"Yeah, she is. The school confirmed it. She was in one of Inverlok's classes. I asked her about her relationship with the professor and she clammed up. I was going to go back to pressure her, but that's when they pulled me off," Stone said.

"You sure it's the same girl?" Nick said.

"Yeah. I brought a copy of the tape. You can see for yourself," Stone said.

"What's her name and address?" Nick said, taking out a pad.

"Roxellana Jameson, 5500 Ellsworth Avenue. One 'a those fancy apartment buildings in Shadyside."

"If she's a student," Sam said, "how does she afford that address?"

"Don't know," Stone said. "That's when they cut me off."

When Sam and Nick finished their lunch with Stone, they called Norton Alexander, a private investigator they sometimes used. He was the replacement of the old reliable gumshoe, Gus Overman, who disappeared two years ago in the midst of a dispute Sam and Nick were having with Scuilli, the district attorney. They had four million dollars that Scuilli thought belonged to him, and he was trying to find them to get it back... and to kill them.

They were hiding out at Overman's hunting camp up north near Dubois. Later they pieced together that Scuilli killed Overman in the process of trying to locate them, but they were never sure and Overman's body was never found. In any event, Alexander, the new guy, was now officially on the job. He was watching Roxellana's apartment, photographing people who came and went, and logging her movements.

After three days Roxellana's schedule became clear. She went out every morning and spent most of the day at school. Two guys that had necks the size of a teenager's waist followed her in their own car. She returned home somewhere between three and five o'clock and a wiseguy of some kind surrounded by more guys with big necks arrived about six. The wiseguy and the necks and Roxellana went out about seven and usually returned between nine and eleven. Sometimes the wiseguy went in afterwards, sometimes not.

Sam and Nick conducted surveillance themselves for the next week, following Roxellana's movements during the day while she was at school. Nothing unusual or suspect emerged. She went to class, had lunch, sometimes went shopping, sometimes went to the library.

In the second day of their surveillance, Maria came up with some information on Roxellana's friends. "Well, I researched the license number of that Lincoln for you," Maria said. "It belongs to the Scarlotti Corporation, and Scarlotti is owned by a guy named Thomas Ilford."

"Who is that?" Nick said.

"According to what I could find out, he's a small time criminal who runs numbers, deals dope and sponsors dog fights."

"Why would a college girl be hanging around with a numbers running drug dealer?" Sam said.

"Beats me," Maria said. "Why don't you ask her?"

The next Monday, Sam joined Roxellana for lunch. She was sitting at a table by herself eating a large Quesadea.

"Mind if I join you," he said.

She looked up from her book, surprised. Then, regaining some balance, sized him up, and said, "Do I know you?"

"No, I don't think so," he said, offering no further commitment or explanation.

"Then why should I let you sit down?" she said, interested in his approach.

"Because you like me?" he said.

"I don't know you," she said.

"That's why you should let me sit down. That way you can get to know me," he said.

"And what if I decide I don't like you after I get to know you?"

"That won't happen," Sam said. "Everybody says I'm likable."

"Okay," she smiled, moving her tray a bit to make room for him to sit across from her with his own tray.

"I'm John," he said.

"Hello, John," she smiled, sensing an opportunity for a conquest. "I'm Roxellana." Under the table, she crossed her legs, bumping him slightly.

"Oh," she said, laughing, "I'm sorry, I think I kicked you."

"It's all right," Sam said, "I've been treated worse."

"You're funny," she said. "Are you a professor?"

"No."

"What's your full name, John?"

"John Donne."

"Oh, you're a poet," she smiled.

"No," he smiled back.

"What then?"

"I look into things."

"Like what?"

"Like your relationship to Professor Inverlok."

She stopped in mid-bite and looked at him intently, trying to figure out what was happening. He was a cop. She was afraid. He knew something about Joey's death. Otherwise he wouldn't be here at the university.

"Oh," she said, stalling for time, "Are you a cop?"

"No."

"Then why should I talk to you?"

"Why not? You got something to hide?" Sam smiled.

"No. What would I have to hide?"

"Good," Sam said, "Nothing to hide. What was your relationship to him?"

"I assume you're here because you know we were lovers," she said.

"Yeah, I know that. That's all?"

"Isn't that enough?" she said.

"How'd he end up dead?" Sam said.

"How would I know?"

Taking a wild leap, Sam said, "You're the last person who saw him."

"That doesn't mean I know what happened to him."

"Was he worried about anything? Did he say anything to you about somebody threatening him?"

"No. He just seemed normal."

"What was your relationship like?"

"Why do you want to know all this. Who are you?"

"I work for somebody who was close to him," Sam lied.

"Who?"

"I'd rather not say more," Sam said. "If you don't know what happened to him, there's no reason not to talk to me,"

"You think I killed him?"

"I think you know what happened to him," Sam ventured.

"Are you married?" she said.

"No."

Roxellana scooted her chair back from the table and sat sideways to the table, crossing her legs and allowing her skirt to come up high on her thighs. Sam watched her move.

"Nice legs," he said, sipping his coke.

"Would you like to go out with me?"

"No."

"Why? Don't you like me?"

"You're very attractive, but I don't go out with people I don't know. They might turn out to be killers."

"That again," she laughed. "You think I might fuck you to death?"

"That wouldn't be too hard," Sam smiled. "I'm an old guy. I might die from the excitement."

"You know, sitting here with me could be dangerous for you," she said.

"How so?"

"My boyfriend is jealous and I don't think he would like you."

"I can't believe he wouldn't like me. I'm a friendly guy. And you're the one who came on to me," Sam said.

"Yeah, but I would tell him you came on to me," she smiled.

"You think he'd beat me up?"

"I know you think you're tough, but my boyfriend is tougher. And he's got guys working for him that are twice as big as you."

"So we've moved from dating to threatening," Sam said. "How did that happen. I thought you were just getting to like me."

Roxellana got up from the table, collected her books, hugged them to her chest and said, "Don't come around me again. I don't like these questions."

"Well, at least it's the questions and not me," Sam smiled.

Sam watched Roxellana walk through the crowded cafeteria and out the door. He followed her at a distance. Her car was parked at an angled slot on the street. Next to her car was a black Lincoln Town Car. Two large men got out of the Lincoln and opened the door of Roxellana's car for her.

Chapter 18

Not everyone suspected that Roxellana was a killer. To Thomas Ilford, she could do no wrong. She was the best thing that had ever happened to him, though he would never admit it, and he was having the time of his life.

That evening, as they were getting ready to go to an anniversary party for Ilford's parents, Roxellana told Ilford about her meeting with Sam.

"I'd feel better if Gino went with you during the day," he said, mixing a drink.

"Tommy, I wouldn't of told you if I thought you'd start that again. I'm not going to go around followed by goons. I told you that. I'm just telling you about this guy because I thought you'd want to know."

"So what'd he ask you about?"

"That college professor that got killed at the dog house. You know, the one who was pestering the dogs. This guy wanted to know if I know how he died," she said.

"How the hell would he know to ask you? How the hell would you know anything about this college professor? This guy askin the questions, he must have some inside information," Ilford said.

"That's what I thought and that's why I told you," Roxellana said.

"But who could he get information from? It's just you and the kid and my guys and me. There's nobody to give him information."

"I know. It's scary."

"I need to find this guy and find out who he is and why he's asking you these questions. I'll have Skeeter work on that right away."

Ilford went into the other room and talked on the phone while Roxellana finished getting dressed. She was wearing a sleek black sheath that hugged her curves, a diamond necklace that Ilford had given her, and she had a black ribbon tying back her long hair.

"Wow," Ilford said, beaming. "You're a knockout."

Roxellana was to be a surprise guest at the anniversary party. Ilford's two brothers would be there with their families and Ilford would be there with Roxellana.

Ilford's father, James Sr., was a successful auto parts dealer. He had several stores and had provided a wealthy, if not sophisticated life-style for his family. Ilford's brothers, Jimmy and Edward, were also successful. Jimmy was an orthopedic surgeon and Edward was a real estate developer. Both the father and his brothers looked down on Thomas, the youngest.

Tom had flunked out of college in his sophomore year. He was bored and resentful at the praise constantly being lavished on his brothers. He was always being told about how brilliant they were, how hard they worked, and how he should be more like them. But Tom decided he would *not* be like them. They would get good jobs, he would get money. They would be respectable, he would be his own man. They would look down their noses at him and he would look down his nose at them.

Except for his mother, Tom Ilford hated his family. But for mom, he would not have attended the anniversary gathering at all. On the other hand, going with Roxellana was a chance to ram it up their respectable asses. Tom was nearly fifty; his brothers were a few years older. Tom had been divorced for some years — another subject of disapproval—but his brothers had stuck it out with the dowdy chubbies that their wives had become. Roxellana would be a welcome addition to that mix, Ilford chuckled.

Roxellana could not have come at a better time for Ilford. He had begun to experience something like a mid-life crisis when she showed up, and he needed a change from the regular routine of take-bets-and-collect-money, with drug dealing on the side. He had begun to despise the people who populated his world of minor league crime, but he didn't know people in any other world. He needed a change, something new, something better, something challenging and exciting. Roxellana.

They arrived at the parents' house at six o'clock, an hour later than his mother told him to come, accompanied by two carloads of thugs, one in front of his Lincoln Town Car, one behind. It was a show of force that he loved and his brothers hated. The thugs waited in the cars out in front of the house as he and Roxellana walked to the front door.

His mother answered the door and could not conceal the surprised look when she saw Roxellana, but she recovered quickly and asked them to come in. Tom introduced Roxellana to his mother, who was gracious in welcoming her, and then turned to the crowd in the living room, the brothers, their wives and various children. Conversation came to a stop as the people seated in the living room realized that Roxellana was Tom's date. Tom had always been outrageous, but this was over the top. With Roxellana on his arm, Ilford walked into the center of the group of brothers, wives, children and his father, and with enthusiasm, introduced Roxellana to the group. The women forced false smiles and his brothers couldn't disguise their interest. Jimmy Sr. maintained a poker face.

There was an awkward moment of silence, and then one of the plump wives, Doreen, said, "Roxellana, come into the kitchen. We can use some help."

Doreen, Roxellana, and the other wife, Belle, scurried into the kitchen followed by Tom's mother.

In the living room, silence prevailed as Tom reached for a handful of peanuts from a bowl on the coffee table.

Finally, Edward said, "Kind of robbing the cradle aren't you Tommy?"

Ilford said nothing, but chewed his peanuts.

"I mean, Tom," Jimmy Jr. said, "this is the folks' anniversary. Don't you think a little respect is in order?"

"Do you think I'm disrespectful, pop?" Ilford said to his father, opening another peanut.

Jimmy Sr. sipped his drink.

"Do you think I'm disrespectful, Edward?" Ilford continued, chewing intently.

"Well, we don't even know this girl, Tom," Edward said.

"Yeah. You don't know her. Is that disrespectful?" Ilford said.

"Shut up, all of you," Jimmy Sr. said. "Enough."

Dinner was on the table a half hour later and conversation seemed to pick up a little, but was still constrained. Ilford noticed his brothers eyeing Roxellana's chest, and he smiled. Doreen and Belle seemed unusually quiet. His mother kept up a running patter. Jimmy Sr. remained quiet.

After dinner, in the kitchen, Roxellana stood at the sink and scraped uneaten food into a plastic bag and then stacked the plates for washing. Belle and Doreen carried dishes from the table and put them on the counter. Ilford's mom sat with the men in the living room. Raised voices were heard in the kitchen occasionally.

As she placed her load of dirty plates on the counter near Roxellana, Belle said, "Don't you think Tommy is a little old for you, dear?"

"No," Roxellana said evenly, "He's just fine."

"He could be your father, you know," Belle continued.

"Yeah, I guess. But he isn't," Roxellana said, continuing her scraping, smiling as she looked sideways at Belle.

"What are you trying to do here?" Doreen said, depositing a load of dirty cups next to the plates. "Are you trying to cause trouble between the brothers? Are you trying to ruin his parents' anniversary?"

Roxellana stopped scraping, turned to Doreen, and said, "I'm not the one who is starting an argument. I just came because Tommy asked me to come, that's all."

"Well, you shouldn't have," Belle said. "It's disgusting. You can see what effect you have on this party. And that dress you're wearing. Now the brothers are bickering too. You can hear them in there. How do you think the parents feel?"

Roxellana dried her hands, left unscraped dishes in the sink, and walked through the dining room into the living room, where a full- blown family discussion was in progress.

Everyone became quiet when Roxellana appeared in the arch leading to the living room. She walked over to Ilford and said, "I don't think I'm welcome here, Tommy. The women in the kitchen said that I have ruined this party and I'd like to go now."

Belle and Doreen now stood in the archway, their arms folded on their chests like executioners whose victim walked away from the block before they got a chance to swing the big axe. Their husbands looked at them as if to ask "what the hell?" The husbands had been enjoying the traditional baiting of their younger brother, pointing out yet one more time, over their mother's protests, his shortcomings and failures and bad taste.

But now their wives had, by their rudeness, turned the girl into a heroine. Now it was the brothers who were in bad taste and Tom and Roxellana were the victims.

Ilford stood up and took Roxellana's arm.

"You're right, Roxellana," he said. "Nobody here seems to happy to see either one of us."

Jimmy said, "Wait a minute. They didn't mean anything. We're all just a little surprised is all."

Edward said, "Yeah, Tommy. You and your squeeze, you should stay."

Roxellana looked at Edward and took a step away from Ilford. "I've had enough," she said. "I'm nobody's squeeze. And you and Jimmy here are just pissed off because you're stuck with those two fat bitches over there. I know men and I can see that you both want to fuck me. Well, that's too goddam bad because fucking me is something your brother does. It's not something you do. You go fuck the cows."

By now, Jimmy Jr. and Edward were on their feet. Roxellana turned to Mrs. Ilford and said, "Thanks for having us." Ilford kissed his mother on the cheek, took Roxellana's elbow, and steered through the crowd to the front door, ignoring his father and his brothers.

Chapter 19

John Derringer and Zorba arrived in Pittsburgh about 2:00 p.m., and Derringer drove to the police station downtown. He parked the truck outside the front door and the disheveled pair walked in. They hadn't washed for several days by this time, and they smelled like it.

"I want to report a murder and an attempted murder," he said to the officer at the desk.

"Which is it?" the officer said, skeptically, trying to figure out how to get upwind.

"Both," Derringer said.

"Wait a minute," the officer said. He phoned a detective who took his time coming out, gathering from the desk man's description that some derelicts had come in the station to get warm. Twenty minutes later he appeared. He took a whiff and backed up a step.

"'Sup?" the detective said, languidly, holding a handkerchief over his nose.

"Murder," Derringer said. "No need to rush out here or anything."

"A bo who stinks," the cop said. "What you mean, murder?"

"That's when one guy kills another guy," Derringer said.

"Yeah, Willie Nelson, I know murder. What you two beefcakes got to do with it?" the detective said.

"Somebody killed our friend," Zorba said.

"You see it?" the cop said.

"Yeah," Zorba said.

"Okay. Come on back here," the cop said, opening a door to a corridor leading to a room full of desks.

The three sat at the cop's desk. The cop opened the window and then said, "Okay, first I need your names. You first."

"Zorba."

The cop looked up with a little smile. "Zorba?"

"Address?"

"None."

"None?"

"None."

"Occupation?"

"Alcoholic."

"Alcoholic?"

"Drunk, if that's better."

"Oh, yeah, drunk, thanks, that's loads better. And you, pal, your name?."

"John Derringer."

"Derringer."

"Yep. Like the gun."

"Address?"

"Cutfahrt bar."

"You live in a bar?"

"Well, yeah, as much as anyplace."

"Occupation?"

"Inventor, architect, mechanic, engineer, chemist, and roofer."

"Employer?"

"Between jobs."

"Oh, yeah, I heard 'a them. Between Jobs. They're over on Boulevard of the Allies, ain't they?"

"Yeah."

"All right yuns, we have Zorba and John Dillinger...

"Derringer."

"We have Zorba and John Derringer, off-time blue-cheesers of no known address or occupation, smelling like ripe garbage, comin' in to report a kiss-off," the cop said.

"That's right," Zorba and Derringer said.

"Whose ticket got punched?"

"Arnie," they both said.

"Oh, yeah. Arnie. Should'a known it wuz Arnie. Who pickled him?"

"Well, it was the dogs, I guess," Derringer said, "but they were Thomas Ilford's dogs."

"Now let me guess. You and Zorba and Arnie had busted inta' Ilford's house, and then them dogs bit the shit out of Arnie and it's a red-blanket kiss-off. That how it happened?"

"No," Zorba said.

"How about this? You and Tom Ilford used to be classmates at the Shadyside Academy and he had you over to the estate to shoot the shit and drink a few cold ones. While you were sittin around yammin' about the yacht and and shit, Ilford decides to have the dogs give Arnie the works," the cop said. "Somethin' like that?"

"No," Derringer said. "They snatched us when we were all drunk-up and took all three of us to a barn and then this Ilford set his dogs on Arnie and killed him. We saw his body."

"How come you know it was Ilford?"

"Because the guy that works for Ilford told us who owned the dogs and what they were doing."

"What do you mean, what they was doing?"

"They were snatching guys like us and taking us out to their farm, where they turned the Pitt Bulls loose to kill us. The farm's out by Apollo."

"Yeah, it's right off Route 819," Zorba said.

"Why would they do that?"

"The guy told us it was because Ilford sells tickets to watch dogs kill people and he makes a lot of money doing it. And he needs people to kill. He thought he'd kill us all, but he only got Arnie."

"Yeah, Arnie. Sure. How'd you two bust out?"

"We figured out what they were doing after they took Arnie away and we heard the dogs and him screaming. So when they dragged Arnie's body out and came to get us in the truck, we jumped them and got away. I got the truck parked right outside the door."

The cop looked startled and said, "You do? You got the truck?"

"Yeah, here's the keys," Derringer said.

"So let me get this straight," the cop said. "You and Zorba here and Arnie got sneezed by Ilford's hard-boys. They take you to a farm off Route 819 where Mr. Ilford's Pit Bulls give Arnie a wood overcoat and you two get away, but not before you take Ilford's boys over the hurdles and get them to tell you who's the whip hand. That about it? Oh, and you got the truck outside," the cop said.

"That's it," Derringer said.

"And this Arnie, he wouldn't have an address or an employer either, would he?"

"Not that I know of," Derringer said, "but they know him at the Cutfahrt."

"Okay gents, I think I got this all down. Let me crunch on it. I guess I can't call you, so I'll give you both my card and you can call me tomorrow and we'll do a layout for you to come in and make a formal say-so."

"Why can't we do that right now?" Derringer said.

"I've got to do some preliminary bust-a-gut first," the cop said, "but when you call me tomorrow, I'll have it all packaged up."

Walking down Grant Street, Zorba said, "I told you it wouldn't work, goin to the cops. They don't believe us."

"I know," Derringer said, "it's the routine stall, but we had to try."

• • •

"This is Mickey Shaunasey," the cop said into the phone, "calling for Mr. Ilford."

"Can I tell him what it concerns, please," the secretary said.

"Police business."

Ilford came on the line. "Tom Ilford."

"Mr. Ilford, this is Mickey Shaunasey. I'm a homicide detective and I thought I'd better call you about a couple of beef-a-ronis who were in here this afternoon. They claim you sneezed 'em, took 'em to a farm and tried to erase their numbers with Pit Bulls. They also claim your dogs actually did pickle one guy, but they got away. In fact, they claim they crashed out in your truck. They gave me the keys. It's right outside the station."

"Oh yeah, I just found out it was stolen. I'll send somebody down right away to pick it up. And these guys, what's their names?"

"One is John Derringer and the other is called Zorba."

"Zorba?"

"Yeah. No addresses on either. No employers. But they both claim to hang out at the Cutfahrt Bar."

"Okay" Ilford said. "I got the picture. Derringer and Zorba. Cutfahrt Bar. Anything else?"

"I gave 'em my card and told 'em to call here tomorrow to come in and make a formal say-so."

"Nothing on paper yet?"

"Nope."

"Good man," Ilford said. "You call me when you got them coming in and I'll take care of the rest."

"Okay, Mr. Ilford. Just thought you'd want to know."

"You were right, Mickey. We'll get you a suit. I'll send a guy over later today."

"Thanks, Mr. Ilford."

Chapter 20

Sam and Maria Llanas parked in the lot at the corner of Forbes and Murray in Squirrel Hill. Sam had a doctor's appointment and Maria was going shopping.

"What are you so worried about, Sam?" Maria asked. "You're fine. The blood tests were good. What's the problem?"

"I just don't feel like myself," Sam said.

"You mean you don't feel like your seventeen year old self," she said.

"Yeah. I guess that's what I mean," he allowed.

Maria's hair was thick and black and she wore it shoulder length. It accentuated her aquiline features, the delicate nose, the heart-shaped face, the full lips.

"Look Sam, I'm a lot younger than you and I can't do the stuff I used to do."

"Yeah, I guess we all slow down."

"Let me ask you this. Can you still shoot a gun?"

"Yeah."

"Can you still throw a punch?"

"Yeah."

"Can you run a city block?"

"Probably."

"Can you hit somebody with a club?"

"I guess."

"So let's see here. What is it you were complaining about?'

"Okay. Okay. Your point is well taken."

"Look, Darling, life isn't perfect. You may not be happy with things, but you're still doing Okay."

"Promise me one thing," Sam said. "When you think I'm not doing Okay you'll tell me."

"Okay. I promise. In the meantime, you've got an appointment with Steven. Good luck," she said, kissing Sam on the cheek. "I'll be over at the Fashion Bug. Come get me when you're through."

"Okay, Maria," he said.

Sam watched Maria's full hips move as she walked away from the car, then turned, smiled at him, and blew him a kiss.

Sam walked into the second floor office of Dr. Steven Horowitz, the doctor he had been using for routine medical problems. The nurse took him right into an examination room and told him to put on the paper robe.

"Hello, Sam," Horowitz said as he came in. The two shook hands and Horowitz unbuttoned his white coat.

"Hi, Steve," Sam said. "How you doing?"

"Good, how are you?"

"Fine, I think," Sam said. "How come the paper suit? I thought we did that last time."

Horowitz sat in a chair as Sam sat on the end of the examining table. "All your blood work came back and it's fine," Horowitz said. "Only thing is that the PSA numbers are a little elevated, so I want to check your prostate again."

Horowitz did the exam and said, "No abnormal swelling. We'll check these numbers again in a few months. You're fine."

"Yeah, well, we talked about that last time," Sam said.

"There's no magic pill, Sam. It's called aging."

The two men shook hands and Horowitz said, "Come back in six months and we'll do some more blood work, just to make sure everything is Okay."

"Thanks, Steve," Sam said. "I'm glad the blood work looked good, but I sure do hate slowing down."

"Slowing down is not worse. It's different. If you're smart, you'll end up doing the same work, just differently," Horowitz said.

Sam was of two minds about slowing down. On one hand, he rather liked being in a new place. It was exciting. On the other hand, he didn't like the new place at all. The old place was just fine.

There had been plenty of times in his life when he thought he would die, and those times just pointed out his vulnerability. This wasn't really any different. He was vulnerable. Vulnerable to age. But he wasn't dead from age. And as long as he wasn't, he would play the hand and be smarter.

Sam walked a block to the Fashion Bug and sat on a bench outside. He looked at his watch. It had been an hour, but Maria hadn't called, so she was still inside.

Unknown to Maria, however, she was about to meet a strange young woman.

• • •

Celeste Bellman was scared, nervous, and beside herself with anxiety. She had gone shopping to take her mind off things, but now she found herself sitting in the dressing room of the Fashion Bug sobbing uncontrollably. Maria was in the changing room next door. She had already selected a pants suit, and now was trying a skirt and blouse combination. She was walking from the mirror in the showroom back to the changing room when she heard Celeste's sobbing in the room next to hers. She stopped outside of the closed curtain for a minute, and then slowly moved the curtain aside. Celeste was sitting on the floor, her head in her hands, quietly crying.

"What's wrong?" Maria said. "Can I help you?"

"Oh," the girl said. She was twenty, skinny, with coal black hair. Her mouth was pleasantly wide, her black eyes large and swollen with crying, and her nose slightly too large for her face.

"No, no. I'm just a little upset. I didn't mean to bother anyone."

"You're not bothering me," Maria said. She walked over and sat on the bench next to the girl, still sitting on the floor. "I'm Maria," she said, extending her hand to the girl. The girl looked up at her and timidly extended her own hand. "I'm Celeste," she said.

"Okay Celeste, let me change out of these clothes and then maybe you'll feel like telling me what's bothering you. It's never as bad as it seems," she said, smiling.

When Maria had changed and was ready to pay for her pants suit, the girl followed her to the cash register and waited while she paid. Outside, Sam was waiting. Maria walked up to him, taking hold of the girl's arm.

"Well," Maria said, "looks like they didn't carry you off in an ambulance." Sam smiled, and the girl now seemed a little sullen. She hadn't anticipated the company of men.

Sam said "hello," but was somewhat aloof. He hadn't anticipated the company of a strange girl. Anonymity was his way of life, and hanging around strangers didn't sit well.

"Look," the girl said, "I've got to go now."

"Where are you going?" Maria asked.

"I don't know, just shopping," Celeste said.

"We just live in Bloomfield, near here," Maria said. "Come home with us and I'll make a big breakfast and then we'll take you wherever you want to go. Give yourself a little break, Okay?"

The girl looked uncertain, almost ready to cry again. Then she said, "Okay."

Maria took the girl by the arm and the three walked back down Forbes Avenue to the public parking garage. Maria kept up a chatter about her new pants suit and other things in the store. Sam walked along behind and said nothing. In the garage, Maria and the girl sat in the back of the Audi and Sam drove home.

The Pacific Avenue house was fifteen minutes away in Bloomfield. Nick met them at the kitchen door and Maria introduced him to Celeste. Maria started lunch in Sam's unit on the ground floor and Nick gave Sam and Celeste cups of coffee. Sam's place had the most modern kitchen of the three units, and, in any case, that's where all the food was. Maria fired up the griddle of Sam's massive Viking stove for a huge cheese and tomato omelet with grits on the side on another burner. She used a dozen and a half egg whites, two egg yolks and three kinds of cheese. The whole thing, when it was folded over on a huge platter, was topped with slices of tomato. Sam made more coffee and Nick put together a salad with Italian peppers and a little tuna fish. The girl sat in a chair.

When everyone was seated and eating, Nick said, "Outstanding omelet, as usual, Maria.

"Wow," Sam said.

"Thanks, guys," Maria said.

Maria looked at the girl and suddenly stopped chewing. "Where did you get those bruises on your neck?" Maria asked. “And there are some more on your arm. What happened to you?”

The girl squirmed in her seat slightly and looked at her plate, making a show of taking a bite of omelet.

Sam and Nick looked at the bruises too, but said nothing. This was Maria’s baby.

“Talk to me,” Maria demanded.

“It’s nothing. Just my boyfriend,” the girl said.

“Does he always do this to you?” Maria said.

“No, he was scared and upset,” the girl said.

“About what?”

“We had a fight. He just grabbed me.”

“Does he do this often?” Maria said.

“No. He’s never done it before. We just had a fight about something he made me do, that’s all. And I told him I was going to run away.”

“Who is this guy.”

“His name is Eric,” the girl said.

“Where does he live?” Maria said.

“Look, I’ve said too much already,” the girl said. “I can’t talk about it any more.”

“It might help if you could tell us more,” Maria said.

“You don’t want to know,” the girl said. “I’m afraid of these people and you don’t want to know about them.”

As they were talking, Ronin, Sam’s Akita, came in the room, wagging his tail. He had been sleeping and keeping a wary eye on things without revealing that he was there. But now he figured there might be some left-over eggs and it was time to make an appearance.

“Oh my God,” the girl said, seeing Ronin for the first time. She froze in position.

“It’s Okay,” Sam said. “It’s just Ronin. He’s waking up and coming out for some eggs.”

Ronin's tail continued wagging and he looked at Celeste with the mournful Akita eyes. Then he walked over and put his huge head in her lap, his tail wagging all the time. Fearfully, Celeste reached down and gently patted his head. Finally, Ronin backed up a bit and lay down near Celeste's chair.

"My God," she said. "He's lots bigger than Pit Bulls."

"Yeah, he's big," Nick said, "but he likes to be scratched behind the ears."

"Now, tell me about this boyfriend and these dogs," Maria persisted.

"I can't. They would kill me and they'd kill you too," she said.

"Why?" Maria said.

"You have no idea. They would come in here with guns and kill you. You don't want to get involved in this," the girl said.

"It sounds like you're in some trouble and maybe we can help you," Maria said.

"All right," the girl said, "you can't help me. So get that out of your mind. Here's what I can tell you. My boyfriend and I, we saw some things we shouldn't have seen, and I'm afraid these guys he works for are going to find out. He took me to a dogfight and we saw stuff there. But if these guys find out, they'll kill us. Are you satisfied now?"

"Why? Why would they kill you?" Maria said.

"I can't tell you that. If you don't care anything about your own life, think of mine," the girl said, exasperated.

"What can we do that would help you?" Sam said.

"Could you give me enough money to get out of town?" the girl sobbed.

"We can do that," Nick said. "We'll help you get out of town. But you tell us what you saw."

Sam and Nick pulled some bills out of their pockets, counted five hundred, and pushed the money over to the girl.

Sam said, “We did our part. Now talk.”

The girl gathered the money, almost trembling. She paused, then she said, “All right. I saw them kill a man. They attacked him with Pit Bulls.”

“When did this happen?” Sam said.

“Two or three days ago,” the girl said. “It was at the Redgate Farm out by Apollo,” she said. “Eric works for these guys — this Ilford — and Ilford set this whole thing up.”

She gathered the money and stuffed it in her purse, wiped her eyes and her nose, and said, “Thanks. You’ve saved my life. I’m going to leave now. I can walk. I know where I am. Thank you.” She patted Ronin on the head one more time, walked across the kitchen to the back door, and left.

Chapter 21

Following their meeting with Celeste, Sam and Nick did some research on the Redgate Farm and discovered that it was owned by the Scarlotti Corporation, the same outfit that owned the Lincoln Town Car that met Roxellana at Pitt.

"So," Sam mused, "Celeste's boyfriend works for Thomas Ilford, and Ilford not only owns the Red Gate Farm, but also the Lincoln that was waiting for our friend Roxellana."

"What the hell does Roxellana have to do with Ilford?" Nick wondered.

"Beats me, but Ilford is an underworld figure and he's giving some sort of protection to Roxellana, the mistress of our client's murdered son."

"Only when he's not running dogfights," Nick said.

"You think there is a connection between this Ilford and Inverlok?" Sam asked.

"Beats me," Nick mused. "But we know he's involved with Roxellana and we know he sets up dogfights. Maybe he was also involved in some way with Inverlok."

"Why does it always work out like this?" Sam said. "Can't any job be easy?"

"Maybe it is easy," Nick said. "Let's go out and have a look at that farm. We might pick up something we need to know."

• • •

Two days later, Sam and Nick lay in high weeds on the edge of the tree line three hundred yards from the barn where Arnie had been killed. Nick surveyed the barn with a spotting scope, Sam with a pair of ten power Swarovski binoculars. They had hiked into the tree line before dawn and taken up a position where they could see the barn. It was midmorning and there had been no movement in the barn.

Half an hour later, Nick nudged Sam. He heard movement. They backed out of their positions and moved slowly and carefully toward the sound. They heard it again. This time it was the sound of paper being crumpled and it was close.

Twenty yards down the tree line they could see a man. He was sitting with his back against a stump and drinking coffee. The bag he had crumpled was next to him on the ground. Nick signed Sam he was going to approach the man from his front and Sam should stay hidden. Sam moved closer, extracted his .45 and took up a braced shooting position. Nick moved silently in a wide circle to Sam's left.

Fifteen minutes later, Nick emerged from the trees facing the man.

"Jesus Christ," Derringer said, raising his hands when he saw the .45 on Nick's belt, "don't shoot."

"Who are you?" Nick said.

"Nobody. I just came here to rest a while," Derringer said.

"Try again, friend," Nick said.

"Look, I know you work for Ilford, but don't shoot me."

"I don't work for Ilford," Nick said.

"Who are you, a cop?"

"Who I am isn't your concern," Nick said. "Who are you?"

"You're a cop. Wouldn't no one else be here," Derringer said. "I'm here because they kidnapped me and took me to that barn over there and killed one of my friends."

"That doesn't explain why you're here," Nick said.

"I went to you guys, but I didn't think you'd do anything about it. I didn't think you'd come out here. I was gonna handle it myself somehow. They killed my friend and they tried to kill me."

"Who is they?"

"Ilford and his men."

"When did this happen?"

"About a week ago."

"How did they kill your friend?"

"They set the dogs on him. The dogs killed him. We could hear him scream and then they dragged his body outside. I saw it. We both did."

"We?"

"Yeah. Me and Zorba. We was in the truck together with Arnie."

"Why didn't they kill you?"

"When they came to get us, I kicked one of them and knocked him out. We overpowered the other one and drove off in their truck. Are you satisfied now? I'm the same guy that made the report."

Nick motioned to Sam. Derringer turned around and saw the grass turn into a man. Sam stood up, too far away to have heard the conversation, and approached, gun in hand.

"It's Okay. This guy claims he was kidnapped and brought here to be killed by dogs. His friend was killed, he says, and he and another guy got away. He went to the cops but figured they wouldn't do anything, and he's here now on his own."

"To do what?" Sam said.

Nick looked at Derringer.

"To figure out how to get back at the bastards," Derringer said.

Sam holstered his .45 and took out his canteen. "Black coffee," he said. "Need a refill?"

Sam convinced Derringer that he and Nick weren't cops, and the three men sat in the grass and talked. Nick listened.

"You're a witness. You know these guys are gonna be after you," Nick said.

"Yeah, I guessed that," Derringer said.

"Had you considered leaving town?" Sam said.

"No. They killed my friend and they aren't going to chase me off," Derringer said.

"What's the point of hanging around and risking your life?" Nick said.

"Well, when I came out here, I thought I might burn that barn down. But it's too far away. I'd sure as hell get caught in the open, so that's out. But this guy Ilford is a drug dealer as well as a dog fighter and killer," Derringer said.

"Yeah," Nick said. "So what?"

"Well, his big operation is in Oakland. I thought maybe I could hurt him through screwing up his drug sales," Derringer said.

"Risky," Nick said.

"Yeah, but what else can I do?"

"You can stay the hell away from this guy," Nick said.

"You guys don't seem to be too concerned about staying away from him," Derringer ventured.

"We do this for a living," Sam said. "We've had a little more practice at this kind of thing than most people."

"Well, I can't walk away from this," Derringer said. "He killed my friend, he would have killed me, and he's probably gonna kill some other people too for these dog fights."

"His man told you he does this on a regular basis?" Sam said.

"More or less. He said Ilford sells tickets to the big wigs for two thousand dollars a seat, so I'd guess he'll need to keep finding people to kill."

"Look, John, we're telling you to leave this alone and get out of town. This guy will kill you if he gets a chance," Nick said.

"I told you. I can't do that. I'm gonna find a way to hurt him. He tried to kill me. I know how to take care of myself. Why are you guys here, anyway?" Derringer said.

"We have a client," Sam lied, "who has been threatened by this Ilford and who told us about these dogfights. She was there when your friend got killed."

"What are you planning to do?" Derringer said.

"We haven't figured that out yet," Sam said. "Right now we're just watching to see what we can find out about this operation."

"Maybe we can pool our information," Derringer said. "I'm gonna be watching too."

"All right," Sam said. "If you're hell-bent on risking your life, here's a card with our number on it. You can call if you get in trouble."

Derringer said, "The card says John Donne. Are you a poet?"

"We're in the personal protection business," Nick said.

"All right," Derringer said, "I'm glad we're on the same side, because this fucker is going to need some personal protection."

Chapter 22

"You wanna turn it down," Skeeter yelled to Eric.

The music was coming from inside the ramshackle house where Eric lived in East Liberty. Skeeter stood on the front porch and shouted through the screen door. Chris Isaak was singing over an old pair of AR speakers at a sound level that literally shook the glass in the windows of the house.

Eric turned the music down and came to the door accompanied by three large Pit Bulls. "Who are you?" he said to Skeeter.

"Ilford sent me to talk to you," Skeeter said.

"Oh yeah. He called. Come in."

Skeeter stepped inside and the screen door squeaked as he opened it. He had to lift one side of the door to get it open. The ground floor of the frame house had three rooms, the living room, a bedroom and the kitchen. Stairs led to what was presumably a bedroom up above. Skeeter moved to a dilapidated leather arm chair and sat. The dogs immediately came up to him and wagged their tails for attention, slobbering on him and each other. Eric nervously fiddled with the stereo system, turning it off altogether, and then he sat on a couch that wobbled under his weight, facing Skeeter.

Apart from the leather chair and the couch, the only other furniture in the room was an elaborate rack holding stereo equipment. The amplifier was a Crown, the tuner a McIntosh, the CD player a Bang & Olufson, and there were various mixers and other decks whose names Skeeter did not recognize.

On the walls, however, were a series of beautifully framed black and white photographs, some as large as 20 x 24, others as small as 8 x 10. All were printed with a range of grays leading into the controlled whites. Two were of a girl, two were of dogs, the rest were of landscapes. Some were sepia with deep chocolate brown-blacks from being processed in a selenium wash.

"You take these?" Skeeter said.

"Yeah. Photography's my hobby," Eric said.

"Your girlfriend?"

"Yeah, that's Celeste."

"She live here?"

"Yeah,... mostly."

"Were you there when Ilford had the dogfight that killed those guys?"

"Yeah, it was my dogs?"

"These dogs right here?"

"Yeah."

"They're not going to attack me are they?"

"No," he laughed. "They only attack because we put 'em in a ring and give them commands. When they're in that situation, they attack. Here, they're just... well, you can see, they're just dogs."

"Was your girlfriend there too?"

"Yeah. What's this about?" Eric was nervous now, but was making an effort to seem relaxed.

"Can I talk to your girlfriend?"

"I guess so. But she's not here right now."

"When will she be back?"

"I don't know. She comes and goes when she pleases. I don't even know where she is."

"From the looks of these photographs, you must be pretty good with a camera."

"Well, I been doin it for a long time. I guess I'm pretty good."

"You ever take any films?"

"What?" Eric said.

"You know, movies," Skeeter said.

"No. I don't take video. It's a different kind of photography."

"So you don't take no films?"

"No."

"How come your girlfriend ain't here?"

"I told you. She comes and goes as she pleases."

"Well, when's the last time she came and went?"

"I don't know. Couple a days ago."

"You don't care about that?"

"No. Why should I?'

"She fuckin somebody else?"

"I don't know what she does."

"Are you tellin me she could be fuckin somebody else and you wouldn't care?"

"Look, I don't know what this has to do with dogfights, but yeah, I would care. If she was doin that she would more than likely just leave."

"More than likely?"

"Yeah."

"You know anything about a letter that Ilford got?" Skeeter said.

"No. What letter?"

"You were there at the meeting the other day. You know. He got a letter with a video tape in it."

"Oh, yeah. That. I forgot."

"You didn't send him that letter, did you?" Skeeter said.

"Hell no. You think I'm crazy?"

"Well, you were there," Skeeter said, watching Eric for a reaction.

"I don't know nothin about that shit, man. You'd get yourself killed doin something like that," Eric said.

"Ain't that the truth," Skeeter said.

Chapter 23

Within a week, Skeeter had interviewed everyone who was in the barn except for Eric's girlfriend, Celeste. Eric said he didn't know where she was, that she would be back. But after all the interviews, Skeeter was no farther along than when he started. Any of the twenty-four people who witnessed the man-killing dog fight could have sent the note. That wasn't going to fly with Ilford. So he needed a name. The only person who emerged at all as a suspect was Eric, and that was only because he had some familiarity with cameras and his girlfriend was AWOL. That wasn't much to go on, but that's all he had.

He'd been avoiding Ilford, but Ilford sent for him and he was waiting in the outer office, nervous, uncertain of what to say. Finally, the secretary nodded and one of the big men on either side of the door opened it. Skeeter went in.

"What'cha got for me," Ilford demanded, seated at his desk.

"Well, boss. I interviewed everybody who wuz there — well, except for one girl — and I don't have much."

"I don't pay you to not have much," Ilford scowled.

Skeeter noticed for the first time since he'd come into the office that they weren't alone. Roxellana was sitting just out of his line of vision in a corner of the room. He didn't really know who Roxellana was except that the boss was apparently screwing her and taking her around places. She was a girlfriend, maybe a whore. He didn't have anything to do with her.

"Who is the girl you didn't talk to?" Ilford said.

"Her name is Celeste. She's the girlfriend of one of the dog handlers, some guy named Eric."

"Why didn't you talk to her?"

"She doesn't live there all the time and I been goin back now and then to see if she'd shown up, but so far she hasn't. I just finished all the other interviews, so now I'll go after her."

"Are you telling me there is no one you suspect out of all these people — how many?"

"Twenty-four."

"No one?"

"Well, one guy seems a possibility. This guy Eric, the dog handler with the missing girlfriend."

"Why?"

"Two reasons. He fools around with cameras and the girlfriend is missing. No one else is missing and no one else seems to have any cameras."

Roxellana got out of her chair and walked slowly over to Ilford. She stood behind him and massaged his shoulders while Skeeter talked.

"Can I say something, Tommy?" she said.

"Sure, Honey. What's up?"

"I know this guy Eric. Remember, I used to live there. And I don't think Skeeter here has it right. Eric is too timid to do something like this. Did you actually talk to Eric, Skeeter?" she said.

"Yes."

"Didn't you see how scared he is? How timid?"

"Well, miss, I didn't really look at that."

Roxellana came around to the side of the desk now, and sat on the edge, facing Skeeter.

"What did you look at?"

"Like I said, just the pictures, the camera stuff."

"That's not much, is it? I mean a lot of people take pictures."

"Well,...Yeah, I guess."

"Did you see any video stuff there? You know, video cameras and tapes and stuff?"

"Well, no."

"What did you see?"

"He just had a lot of really nice pictures on the walls and he said he took pictures."

"He told you that?"

"Yeah."

"Did he tell you he took videos? Films?"

"No."

"Do you know the difference between still photography and video?"

"Yeah, I think."

"What is it?"

"One's movics and the other is pictures."

"And you saw pictures?"

"Yeah."

"But you didn't see movies?"

"No."

"And he told you he didn't take movies."

"Yeah."

"Then why, exactly, do you think he is your best suspect?"

"Well, I....I...."

"Let me ask you this, Skeeter, if I told you that I used to live with this guy Eric, would you think I was a suspect too?

"All right," Ilford interrupted, "That's enough, Honey."

"No, it's not, Tommy. You pay this guy good money to find something out and he comes back with shit. That's what it is, isn't it, Skeeter?"

"Well, Miss, it's what I got."

"Do you think I'm a suspect, Skeeter," Roxellana hissed.

"Come on, now miss, I didn't say nothin like that."

"No, tell me, Skeeter. Am I a suspect?"

"Well, if you lived with the guy,..."

Roxellana smiled. "I'm no fortune teller, Skeeter," Roxellana cooed, "but I'd like to see your hands. Put them here on the desk."

Skeeter looked at Ilford as if to get direction as to what to do. Ilford shrugged. Skeeter scooted up to the edge of his chair and put his hands on the desk, palms down. Roxellana moved off the edge of the desk and took a step toward the seated man.

"Look at me," she commanded.

As he looked up at her, she pivoted her right hip toward the hapless Skeeter and plunged a letter opener into the back of his right hand. It went through the back of his hand and thunked into the wood of the desk. The sound of the blade hitting wood preceded Skeeter's bellow by milliseconds. Shouting in pain, Skeeter jumped from his chair, reaching with the other hand to pull the letter opener out by the handle. Ilford sat up in amazement, and after the initial shock, a slight smile played on his lips.

"Don't you ever accuse me, you sonofabitch," she said. "You understand?"

She stood in front of him, her legs spread belligerently, hands on her hips, staring at him with hatred.

"Yes, miss," he whispered, cradling his hand, the bloody letter opened still sticking through it, tears welling up in his eyes, his face contorted in pain.

Ilford was standing, his jaw dropped in amazement. He paused, then said, "You better get that looked at, Skeeter, and then you interview that girl."

"Yes, boss," Skeeter said, backing out of the office. He pressed his injured hand against his chest, blood from the wound staining the wrinkled pin stripe suit and the cheap tie.

Roxellana smiled at Ilford and walked around to where he stood, lifted herself on the edge of the desk, her skirt well up on her shapely thighs, and said, "I'm sorry, Tommy, but he shouldn't of said that." Ilford collected composure as best he could, licking his lips and smiling.

"That's okay, Honey. He'll get over it. In the meantime, I think he has the message that we need some results."

Ilford's hand ran up the shapely thigh and disappeared under the skirt.

Chapter 24

Eric Calder and Celeste Bellman walked the three large Pit Bulls. It was a bad part of town, but no one bothered them. The dogs took up the whole sidewalk the way a tank occupies a two-lane road. Celeste had gone back to Eric as soon as she left Sam's kitchen. There was hope for both of them now. She had enough money so that they could both get in the truck and leave.

"I've got some money now, Eric. Let's get the hell out of here," she said. "This isn't working out. When Ilford finds out what you and your old girlfriend have done, he'll kill us all."

"We can't run. They'd know it was us if we run now," he said.

"This was a bad idea. I don't know how you thought you could do this," she said, tugging at the leash of the dog she was walking.

"Ilford's been trying to find out who sent the film, and one of his guys came to talk to me," he said.

"He did? Jesus. Does he know?" she said, stopping in the middle of the sidewalk.

"Come on. No. He doesn't know. But he asked me about the prints and my cameras."

"Why?"

"I don't know. He also asked about you. He knows you were there when the guy got killed," he said.

A group of teenagers crossed the street to avoid the dogs, and the dogs looked suspiciously at the group. The dogs had claimed the sidewalk as their own, as dogs will do, and snuffled satisfaction that their territory had not been invaded. They continued on without interruption sniffing stop signs, telephone poles and the odd patches of grass.

"Damn, Eric. You didn't tell me that," she said.

"Hell, Celeste, I haven't seen you for two days. How could I tell you?"

"They're gonna kill us. That's all. They're gonna kill us," she stammered.

"They're not gonna kill us, Celeste. They don't know anything. And they won't," he said.

"Eric, I don't want to do this any more. We got to get rid of this tape. Just forget about it. Maybe they'll never find out who sent it."

"I'm Okay with that. When we get back home, I'll give you the tape and you take it somewhere and throw it in the river. We need to get it out of the house. If that guy was to come back right now and search the house, he'd find it."

"Okay. As soon as we get back I'll take it and throw it off a bridge," she said.

"Yeah. If they can't find the tape and we don't make any more demands, they'll never know who sent it," he said.

"Yeah, but what about Roxellana? She'd never agree to get rid of the tape," Celeste said.

"Yeah, I know. But we'll just do it," he said.

"She'll go nuts when she finds out," Celeste said. "She may even tell Ilford you thought it up and get you killed."

"Nahh."

"Don't be stupid, Eric. You remember what you told me about her father. She'd do anything."

"We'll just have to cross that bridge when we come to it," he said. "For right now, let's just get rid of the tape."

"Okay," she said.

Once they had decided to free themselves from the threat of Ilford's finding out that they were involved, their moods both brightened. The specter of death was banished and the rest of the walk was enjoyable. The dogs tugged at the leashes and romped with each other and sniffed everything they could get near. Life was beautiful. They wouldn't be killed after all.

But things changed when the pair rounded the corner by Eric's dilapidated house. A man that neither of them had ever seen sat behind what was left of the rotted railing on the front porch. The door was open and other men seemed to be inside.

Eric turned to Celeste. "Jesus Christ, they're here already. We got to act now before they find the tape. We got to do this right now. The tape is in the freezer. It's with the ice cubes. You say you're going to make us cold drinks. You slip the tape out of the freezer when you get ice cubes and take off in the truck."

"Okay," she said uncertainly.

"You got to do it, Celeste. Otherwise, they'll find it and they'll kill us both."

When they approached the front porch, the man stood up and held up his hand. "You wait out here," the strange man growled.

The dogs alerted to his aggression and stood stiff legged five yards away, looking at him.

Eric had to get inside before they found the tapes. He had to get past this guy. He needed to find courage he didn't really have. The dogs. That was it. Use the dogs.

"This is my house," Eric said. "and I'm going in there. If you think you can deal with these dogs without getting hurt, get in my way."

The man went inside and Eric could hear loud talking. Eric walked on the porch, handed the leashes to Celeste, and went into the living room. Skeeter, his hand in a large white bandage, sat in the only chair in the living room while another man ripped CD's off the shelves and scattered them on the floor. Photographs were already in a heap of broken frames in the middle of the floor and the couch had been slit with a knife. Celeste came in with the dogs and handed the leashes to Eric.

"Goddam it Rocco," he yelled. "I told you to keep them out of here," staring at Eric and Celeste and the dogs.

"I don't know what you're looking for or who told you could do this, but whatever it is, you don't have to break everything while you're looking," Eric said.

"Is this the girlfriend?" Skeeter leered.

"Yeah, and she's going to make us a couple of cold drinks. We been walking these dogs for the last hour."

Celeste brushed past the big man who was still pulling CD's off shelves, handed the leashes to Eric, and went to the kitchen. She got two glasses out and went to the freezer, where she got the tray of ice cubes. At the first opportunity, she slipped the tape into her jacket pocket, filled the glasses with lemonade, and took them into the front room. She handed one to Eric and looked uncomfortably at Skeeter.

"So, sweetheart, did your boyfriend tell you about the mail that Mr. Ilford got?" Skeeter said.

"Yes," she said.

"And?"

"And nothing. I don't know nothing about it," she said.

"But you were there?" Skeeter said, nursing his bandaged hand.

"Where?"

"At the dogfight. Where else?"

"Yes."

"Do you have any idea who might have done this?"

"No. I was there, but so were a lot of other people. I don't know nothing else."

"Maybe you'd remember better if Rocco asked you?" he sneered. "Rocco, he likes brunettes."

"I'm getting some more lemonade," she said, pushing past the big man, who was heading into the bedroom to start his destruction there.

Alone in the kitchen, she opened the refrigerator door, poured the lemonade, replaced the bottle, snatched Eric's truck keys off the kitchen table, and walked out the kitchen door. She walked straight to Eric's old Toyota Tacoma truck, started the motor, and threw it in reverse. Skeeter heard the truck start and jumped out of his chair, turning in time to see the truck backing out of the yard and onto the street.

"Goddam it, Rocco," he yelled. "Get your ass off that porch and stop her. Stop that bitch."

Skeeter wheeled to face Eric, his face contorted with rage, and found himself looking at three large Pit Bulls who were now growling.

"Back those fucking dogs up," he yelled at Eric. "Carl, get the fuck in here. Shoot 'em."

"These dogs belong to Mr. Ilford," Eric said.

"Then get them out of my way," he yelled. Carl stood in the doorway of the kitchen with a 9mm Glock in his hand.

"Back," Eric commanded. "Down." The dogs backed up and lay down.

"You can step over them now," Eric said to Skeeter. "But move slowly or they'll think you're attacking them."

Skeeter stepped gingerly over and between the three dogs, and motioned to Carl, still standing in the door with his gun, and headed for the front door. Rocco was standing helplessly at the curb, having failed to stop the girl in the truck.

"Drive the fucking car, Rocco," Skeeter yelled. "Do you think you can do that?"

The three men piled into the Lincoln Town Car and headed after Celeste. When they got to the first stop sign, the truck was visible several blocks ahead. The Lincoln spun into a right turn and accelerated after the truck. Rocco slowed for the stop signs and then raced through in pursuit of the rusted pickup.

Eric's truck entered Penn Circle in East Liberty and took off as fast as it could go on the four-lane circular road. Celeste roared past the East Liberty police station and cut right on Penn Avenue. The Lincoln was two blocks behind her.

At the intersection of Penn and Negley, traffic was stopped ahead of Celeste at a red light. She bounced the truck up on an island and steered past the six or eight cars stopped ahead of her. She flew down off the island and roared across Negley against the light, narrowly missing collision with other cars, their horns blaring as they tried to avoid her unexpected interruption of their right of way.

The Lincoln couldn't follow her up on the island and had to wait through the light behind the line of cars ahead of it. Rocco laid on the horn and nearly rear-ended the car in front of him when the light changed. Finally, Rocco got through the light, but Celeste, now had a comfortable lead. She turned off Penn Avenue and roared down Pacific Avenue. The throttle was on the floor but

Celeste had no notion of the throttle. She just wanted the damned truck to go faster. She was scared and she was running for her life. The truck was in second gear, near redline, with the engine screaming like a pig-fed Muslim and belching enough blue smoke to obscure the entire neighborhood.

Celeste roared down Pacific until she got near the end, where it intersects with Liberty Avenue. There, she wheeled the truck up over the curb and into the lawn of a four story brick Victorian house. A Landcruiser was just backing out the driveway as she tore ruts in the front yard and skidded to a stop by the front porch.

Sam looked out the side window of the Landcruiser at the pickup truck that had just plowed ruts in his front yard and said, "What the hell?"

The Lincoln was now close behind, bouncing and yawing down Pacific Avenue after Celeste, and it lurched to a stop in front of the house. Doors flew open and three men piled out of the Lincoln and moved briskly toward the truck. The girl was out of the truck and up the three steps to the front porch, where she was pounding on the door.

The three heavies cut across the front yard in a direct line to the porch, but Sam intercepted them in front of the steps.

"Stop there," Sam said loudly. Sam stood between Skeeter and the first step.

"Out of the way, hayseed," Skeeter said, reaching out with his good hand to push Sam out of the way.

Sam pocked the straight-arm and punched the bandaged hand with a solid cross that came from the waist.

"Owwwwwwwww. Goddam it, you sonofabitch," Skeeter gasped as he fell to his knees, collapsing in pain.

Rocco and his companion Carl were right behind Skeeter and Carl moved to step around the fallen Skeeter to get at Sam. Sam saw what was coming and moved to the side to shove Skeeter's kneeling body into the big man's legs, but he checked the move when he saw Carl hesitate. Over his shoulder, he heard the unmistakable low growl of Ronin. That explained the look in the big man's eyes.

Maria was standing on the porch now, her arm around the terrified girl, and Ronin was poised on the top step, just behind Sam, crouching, growling his low growl, the one he used right before he killed something, and looking directly at the big man, waiting for him to touch Sam. Carl saw the danger and backed up. Then Nick appeared in the door with a pump shotgun at his shoulder and plan B involving the use of the Glock on the dog went the way of plan A.

Sam lifted Skeeter roughly to his feet and shoved him against the front fender of Eric's truck. Skeeter held his bandaged hand in his good hand and hissed, "You don't know who you're messing with, you fucker. Get out of my way. You'll end up dead."

Sam grabbed the hand and squeezed it. Again, Skeeter bellowed and dropped to his knees. Tears came to his eyes and froth appeared at his mouth.

Sam picked him up again. He glared at Sam through the tears running down his cheeks.

"You want to say something else," Sam said.

Skeeter said nothing. His face was wet with tears and spittle. Sam could hear his teeth grinding. Ronin's menacing growl was louder now and very large canine teeth were showing. Maria kept her arm around the girl and turned her around to walk into the house, but as the girl turned, the tape fell out of her purse, where it had been hastily placed, and clattered on the cement floor of the porch. She looked at Skeeter, saw instantly that he knew, and bent to pick it up, then went inside with Maria.

"You ever hear of Mr. Ilford," Skeeter hissed, wiping the tears away with his good hand.

"I heard of him," Sam said.

"Well, I work for him and if you know what's good for you you'll give me that girl and that tape. Otherwise, you may not live through the day."

"You and your friends should leave now," Sam said. "If I see you here again, I'm going to hurt you."

Skeeter huffed, backed up, held his bad hand with his good, and motioned with his tear-stained face to his men to return to the car. The knees of his slacks were grass-stained and ripped. The three men looked unhappy as they got into the Lincoln and lurched away, spinning tires on gravel.

Sam talked briefly to Nick, who remained on the porch with the shotgun at his shoulder, now in the low-ready position. Moments later, Maria and the girl appeared at the front door, got into the Landcruiser with Sam and drove off. The Personal Protection Group had contingency plans for events such as this.

Chapter 25

Sam, Nick, and Maria owned two houses and a warehouse in the Pittsburgh area plus the house where they lived. The city safe house was a row house in the Bloomfield section of the city, but it came equipped with a four-car garage that was separate from the house and connected to the house through a tunnel. The house also featured a high tech burglar alarm system and video surveillance. The basement contained a safe room with an escape hatch that opened into a tunnel leading to a city sewer line. The safe room doors were six-inch-thick steel with deadbolts on all four corners. The room was used mostly to store firearms and explosives.

The third house was ten miles from the city in a wooded area. The house sat on a rock bluff overlooking a field, three hundred yards from the nearest two lane road. It had windows, but it looked like a bunker more than anything. It too was equipped with an alarm and video systems that monitored a mile square area around the house. Additionally, it had steel shutters that could be electronically lowered on all windows. The walls were two feet thick and were filled with rebar and cement. Vehicles could be driven into an underground area beneath the house. Heavy weaponry and explosives were stored five hundred yards from the house in an underground bunker that was reachable only from a concealed door in the house.

The warehouse was on the south side of Pittsburgh. It was four stories high. The first floor was rented out to an iron welding shop. The upper floors were accessible through a separate industrial door that opened onto a vehicle-accessible ramp leading to the second floor. There were living spaces and the second and third floors and the fourth floor was used as a large workshop area. It had air compressors, lathes, power saws, and drill presses.

Sam now drove to the Bloomfield house. The partners had completely remodeled the house. It was a row house, but it sat on a corner, so only one wall was a party wall. That wall was reinforced with two inch steel plate and a row of rebar filled concrete blocks from basement to roof. There were three bedrooms on the third floor as well as three bedrooms and two baths on the second. Additionally, there was an emergency chute accessed by a fire pole that people on either the second or third floors could slide down to the basement. The fire pole passage was enclosed on the first floor so that people from the upper floors could bypass a first floor intruder without being shot or seen on their way down.

Sam pulled into the four-car garage and closed the industrial steel door behind him electronically. Sam and Maria led Celeste into the house through the tunnel. The tunnel led to a basement foyer, and stairs from the basement opened into the kitchen, which was beautifully equipped and spacious enough to accommodate a table, where Sam and Nick often sat while Maria cooked.

The living room and an office room made up the rest of the first floor. The living room had windows on two sides and two large Tabriz rugs on the floor. The furniture was comfortable, chairs and couches, tables and lamps, magazines in racks and books in bookcases. Norm Shum black and white photographs lined the inside walls.

"Make yourself at home," Maria said.

"Would you like something to drink?" Sam asked.

"Coffee would be nice," Celeste ventured.

"That's my area," Sam said. "Sounds like a good idea." He began putting some grounds in the electric pot.

"I'm going to call Groceria for some dinner stuff," Maria said. And then to Celeste, "This is a small Italian community and they know us here. So we call the Italian grocery store for groceries and they deliver them. That way we don't have to go out when we think people might be looking for us. Which is by way of saying, you're safe here," she smiled.

"Thank you for doing this," Celeste said. "I don't know why I came to your house. I just didn't have any place else to go and all I could think of was your big dog."

"Pretty good thinking," Sam said.

"Where's Nick?" the girl said.

"He's closing the house up. He and Ronin will be here later," Maria said.

"I was so scared. But now I've caused you to leave your house," the girl said. "I'm so sorry."

"Don't worry about it," Sam said. "We've done it before. That's why we have two houses."

"Who are you?" the girl asked. "Most people don't have two houses and most people don't stand up to people like those guys who chased me."

"We're in the personal protection business," Sam said. "And sometimes we need to have a place to go for our clients, just like you, when people are trying to hurt them."

"Wow. That's awesome," the girl said. "But I can't pay you. The only money I have is what you gave me."

"Don't worry about it," Sam said. "But you're going to have to tell us what we're up against now."

"I guess they're already trying to kill me, so I may as well tell you. My boyfriend works for Thomas Ilford, and Ilford owns the farm where they had that dogfight I told you about."

"I know," Sam said. "Nick and I have already been out there."

"You have?"

"Yeah, after you told us about the dogfight, went out to look at the farm."

"Jesus. I hope no one saw you."

"No one saw us. But we ran into somebody else who knows about the dogfight and the killing."

"Who? You mean one of the other guys who works for Ilford?" the girl said.

"No. He's one of the derelicts they kidnapped and who got away."

"Jesus, I forgot all about them. They did get away. That's why they only killed one man that day," the girl said. "Ilford chased them, but somehow they got away."

"We know that Ilford wanted to kill these guys, but we don't know why he would want to kill you. You're the girlfriend of one of his employees. What did you do?"

"My boyfriend got involved with this girl, Roxellana. She's Ilford's mistress now, but when Eric met her, he and I were living together. Then Eric started fucking her and I moved out."

Sam and Maria looked at each other.

"Roxellana," Maria said. "That's an unusual name. What's her last name?"

"Jameson, I think," Celeste said.

"Do you know this girl?" Sam asked.

"Yeah, I met her when Eric did, and I saw her in the bar quite a bit before she actually started fucking Eric."

"Okay, go on," Maria said.

"After I moved out, this Roxellana bitch lived with Eric for a while, and then somehow she started fucking Ilford, and she became the new queen of crime," Celeste sneered.

"What does she have to do with the dog thing?" Maria said.

"One day after she had been balling Ilford for a while, she called up Eric and told him about this plan she made up to film Ilford at the dogfight where someone gets killed and then shake him down for a hundred thousand dollars. They tell him that if he pays the hundred thousand, they won't send the film to the newspapers."

"How does she know about these dogfights?"

"She knows everything. In fact, Eric tells me she's the one that came up with the idea of having dogs kill a man. She's got Ilford twirled around her finger. According to Eric, Ilford believes everything she says. She's got some crazy ideas, though."

"What do you mean?"

"After she lived with Eric a few weeks, she told him she was balling one of her professors and she was shaking him down for money because she filmed them having sex. He paid or she turned over the film to the guy's wife."

"What was the professor's name?" Sam said.

"I don't know. Eric didn't say," she said. "But he did tell me that Ilford's guys killed him."

"What?" Sam blurted out.

Celeste looked at him in surprise.

"Sorry," Sam said. "Go on. You said they killed the professor."

"Yeah, Eric said he came to the house to pay Roxellana her hush money, but when he got there, he went nuts and Eric called Ilford's men and told them this guy was threatening the dogs. They came and killed him. Then they took his body away and left. I guess Ilford was pretty mad about it and he came over to Eric's house. That's when he met Roxellana, and she ended up leaving with him."

"Why'd they kill the professor?" Maria said.

"I don't know. Eric said it just got out of hand. They came in and he was tearing up the house, and they just went nuts," Celeste said.

"So Eric and this Roxellana witnessed a murder," Sam said. "Aren't they worried about that?"

"Yeah, Eric is. He's scared shitless. But I guess Roxellana thinks she's safe because she's fucking Ilford."

"So she came up with the idea of blackmailing Ilford because she was good at blackmailing people," Maria said.

"Yeah. But it wasn't only the professor. It was also her own father. She told Eric that she thought up this film thing with the professor because she used it on her father. He wouldn't give her money and a car, so she got him drunk and fucked him, then showed him the tape of her fucking him. He gave her the money and the car and she didn't send the film to his boss."

"Jesus," Sam said.

"Yeah, and then he killed himself."

"She told this to Eric?" Maria said.

"Yeah."

"How do you fit in?" Sam said.

"After the Crime Queen forced him to film the dogfight, Eric called me. He was too scared to do it and he was too scared to run away. He knew Ilford would kill him if he found out, but she told him if he didn't do it, she would tell Ilford that Eric came to her with the idea to shake Ilford down. So Eric asked me to run the camera using a remote control while he was working the dogs. He taped the camera up in the barn the day before and it was invisible. All I had to do was push the button when the fight started."

"You saw the fight and the man get killed and then you mailed the tape to Ilford," Maria said.

"I didn't mail it. Eric told me Roxellana mailed it."

"So why were Ilford's guys chasing you?" Sam said.

"When Eric and I got home from walking the dogs, Ilford's men were there tearing up the house. They were trying to find out who was shaking Ilford down. They hadn't yet found the tape. It was in the freezer. So I grabbed it and ran away. That's when they chased me."

"How did they know to look at Eric's house for the tape?" Maria said.

"I don't know. I just assume they were looking for the tape. There was no other reason for them to be there." Celeste said.

"Where is this tape now?" Sam said.

"It's right here," she said, pulling it out of her purse.

Chapter 26

"I couldn't do nothin, Skeeter," the big man called Carl said as he drove the Lincoln. "That fuckin dog was big as a house and he was crouched up there on that porch just lookin at me and growlin. By the time I got my gun out, that other guy come out with the shotgun."

"Just shut the fuck up," Skeeter hissed, nursing his throbbing hand and rocking back and forth in the front passenger seat. "Get the fuck over to that kid's house. He's probably got another tape in there."

The Lincoln leaned and yawed around corners, squealing tires, as it headed toward the East Liberty dog house where Eric raised the killer Pit Bulls. Rocco sat in the back seat and said nothing. Skeeter cursed and yelled at every corner. "That fucker's gonna pay," he threatened, "Whoever the fuck he is, he's dead."

The Lincoln pulled up to the curb and the three men piled out. Skeeter walked to the house, slamming the screen door into the wall, and holding his pounding hand. Inside, Eric, was sweeping up broken glass and stacking up scattered CD's.

Skeeter grabbed him by the neck with his one good hand and pushed him up against the wall. He said, "You little fuck. I saw the bitch drop the tape when I was chasing her. I know it was you. Where are the other tapes?"

Rocco and Carl stood to the side while Skeeter squeezed Eric's neck as best he could with his one good hand.

Eric was scared. They'd seen the tape. What the hell had happened? It looked like she'd got away. He didn't have any other tapes.

"Look man, I don't know what you saw, but I don't have no tapes," he said, squeaking because of the pressure on his throat.

He began to choke in Skeeter's one-handed grip and put his hands up to his head reflexively, but Carl hit him in the ribs and he fell to the floor.

"Give it up," Skeeter growled. "Or we'll bust you up in ways you can't imagine."

The three Pit Bulls had come into the front room when Skeeter burst into the house and grabbed Eric. They were lined up along the far wall now, emitting low growls. Eric could see that no matter what he did, even if he had another tape, he wasn't going to make it though this. He had to escape and the dogs were his only possible avenue for that. He had to act before the goons decided they should lock the dogs outside.

"Okay," he whispered to Skeeter. "I'll tell you what you want to know. Don't hit me any more."

"All right, punk," Skeeter hissed.

Eric got to his feet, rubbing his throat and stalling, and then he yelled, or rather squawked as loud as he could, "Attack."

As if they were on springs, the three Pit Bulls leapt on the three men. One dog locked on Rocco's thigh; the other seized Carl's calf muscle. The third dog went for Skeeter's bandaged hand. Once the dogs were on the men, the growling and screaming ramped up quickly.

Both big men were pounding on the dog's heads as the dogs gripped their legs. But Pit Bulls have locking jaws, and dislodging the bite was not something that could be done with fists, no matter how powerfully they hit.

The dog on Rocco's thigh was shaking his head, driving his teeth ever deeper into the leg, and finally he bit into the sciatic nerve. Instantly, Rocco went down like a bag of bricks. As soon as he was on the floor, the dog went for his face. Rocco held him off with his arms and punched him repeatedly in the face, blows that would have broken all the bones in a man's face, but the dog growled, snapped, and latched onto Rocco's forearm.

Carl was limping and howling as he drug his Pit Bull around the room, bumping into furniture and knocking all of the stereo equipment off its shelving, thrashing and struggling with the dog on his leg. He picked up a turntable and smashed it on the dog's head, but it didn't seem to make any difference. The dog continued to bite and shake his head, and by now his teeth were against the bone.

Skeeter was screaming because the dog was dragging him across the floor by his injured hand. He had tried to fend the dog off with his good hand, but the dog was too strong. It brushed right past the block, knocked him down, and locked on the bandaged hand. Skeeter scrambled frantically to keep up with the dog to take pressure off the hand, but the dog gave him no quarter and shook the injured hand at every opportunity. Skeeter thought he heard bones crunch and screamed, ready to pass out from the pain. He was just about to try to jam his fingers into the dog's eyes when his ears exploded.

Blam, blam, blam, blam, blam, blam, blam, blam, blam, blam, right next to his ear. Carl had got his gun out and shot the dog that had been locked on his leg, and then he had dropped to the floor and put five rounds into the dog on Skeeter. Skeeter's dog released its grip, but it wasn't dead. The dog on the fallen Rocco was terrified by the gunfire. It released its bite on Rocco's forearm and ran out the front door. No one could hear anything from the terrific concussion of shots fired within the small room.

Both big men were bleeding from their legs and arms, their pants and jackets ripped nearly to shreds, and Skeeter's hand was hanging, bleeding, bones exposed, the bandage ripped off the hand completely, with only pieces of tape still on his wrist. Skeeter turned with pure, homicidal hatred to Eric, rolling over on the floor to go at him with his good hand. But Eric was beyond that. He had been shot twice in the chest with 9mm hollowpoints and was dead.

Chapter 27

The intercom buzzed. Ilford picked it up, listened, and said, "Send the bastard in."

Skeeter walked in looking like a human disaster. His entire right arm was in a cast to a point just above the elbow, his face was smudged with grime and his pants were ripped and grass-stained. Part of his palm and his fingers stuck out of the cast, but they were discolored by betadine and were heavily bandaged. The arm-cast was bent and hung in front of his body on a sling.

"What the fuck?" Ilford said.

"Your dog handler. You know, that kid, Eric. He set the dogs on us. Me and Rocco and Carl. Those two are still in the hospital. The dogs busted my whole hand."

"How did that happen?" Ilford said, incredulous.

"We went back to the kid's house to question him about the video tape," Skeeter said. "But he wasn't there and so we began to toss the house. We was goin through the house, lookin for the tape, you know, when the kid and his girlfriend comes home with the dogs," Skeeter said.

"Okay," Ilford said.

"The kid comes in and says the girl's gonna get them a cold drink because they been walkin the dogs. So she goes to the refrig and comes back with two drinks, and I start asking her questions. She starts getting pissy with me and goes back to the refrig. Then, while I wasn't looking, she slips out the back door and runs to the kid's truck and drives off."

"Did you chase her?" Ilford said.

"Hell yes," Skeeter said. "We all three got in the car and chased her, but she had a good start on us and she ended up at some big house in Bloomfield. Drove right up on the lawn and jumped out of the car."

"What house is this?" Ilford said.

"I don't know, but two guys and a wetback woman live there and she must know 'em, cause she banged on the door and they let her in."

"What did you do?" Ilford said.

"We ran out of the car, chasin the girl, and this guy gets out of his car in the driveway and gets in my way. Rocco and Carl are behind me and we're next to the girl's truck in the middle of this guy's yard."

"So what then?" Ilford said.

"The girl is on the steps with the wetback woman and as she starts to go inside, a tape drops out of her purse and falls on the porch. Then this guy steps in front of me. I tell him to get the fuck out of my way and he grabs my bad hand and punches the hell out of it. I thought I'd pass out," Skeeter said.

"So I get up and he punches it again. Carl is about to go around me to take him out when this huge fuckin dog shows up crouched on the porch, growlin and lookin straight at Jub like he's gonna kill him. So Carl backs up to shoot him but some other guy comes out on the porch with a shotgun. That's when we left," Skeeter said.

"Who are these guys?" Ilford said. "Somebody's muscle?"

"No. I don't know who they are. But they got guns and a dog big enough to double as a horse."

"I want to find out who these guys are," Ilford said.

"He's nobody I ever seen."

"I guess the girl knew who he was, though," Ilford said. "Maybe he's the one sent the tape to me. Maybe he's behind the whole thing."

"Could be. Like I said, a tape fell out of her purse while she was on the porch with this woman."

"So you tossed Eric Darin's house and then the two of them come home and then the girl runs out and drives away and goes to the house of the mystery man and drops a tape on the porch. That what happened?" Ilford said.

"Yeah. More or less," Skeeter said.

"So you fuck up at Darin's house and then you fuck up again at this mystery man's house, and he busts you up to boot," Ilford sneered.

"He didn't bust me up," Skeeter said. "It was them fuckin dogs," Skeeter huffed.

"What dogs?" Ilford said.

Things weren't going well, Skeeter thought. Now comes the bad part.

"We couldn't do any more with the girl, so we went back to the kid's house to finish searching. When we walk in, he sicks the dogs on us," Skeeter said.

"Go on," Ilford said. "I think I see another fuck-up coming."

"It wasn't a fuck-up, Mr. Ilford. We was fightin for our lives. Those dogs are killers. You know that. And they was on us. All of us. Even Rocco couldn't get the dog off him. He hit him with everything he could find, but the dog was still on him. Finally, Carl got to his gun and shot two of the dogs and the other one ran out the door."

"You shot my dogs," Ilford said very slowly and distinctly, shifting his weight to the front of the chair. "You shot my dogs."

"Yes sir," Skeeter said. "And the kid, he took two to the chest. He's dead too."

Ilford looked at him and said nothing. He face worked. His lips moved, lightly rubbing against each other. His eyes narrowed. His teeth were clenched.

Skeeter looked at Ilford, who glared at him with eyes that came from another galaxy. "Get out before I kill you," Ilford hissed.

Skeeter headed for the door. Quickly. It closed behind him. Ilford stared at the closed door.

Chapter 28

Sam, Nick, Celeste and Maria watched silently as the dogs ripped Arnie to death. At first he was able to kick at them, but the dogs quickly broke him down with bites to the knees and ankles. Once he was down flat, they were on him. One was at his head, another at his legs, the third at his stomach and chest. His arms flailed helplessly and his screams were quickly drowned out by the increasing intensity of the growling. When the tape ended, Arnie was a motionless bloody lump with no face.

"Jesus," Maria said.

"How did people react to this?" Nick said.

"I don't know. I think everybody was just in shock," the girl said. "It was real quiet after he was dead. The only thing you could hear were the dogs snarling and ripping sounds when they got hold of some piece of clothing that had not yet been ripped off."

"What did Ilford do?" Sam said.

"He had to yell at Eric and the others to get the dogs. They were dragging the body all over the ring and tearing big chunks of flesh out of it. The boys were just standing there. I guess they were shocked like the rest of us."

"What happened then?" Nick said.

"The boys got the dogs off the dead guy and they started wiping them off. They were all covered with blood and stuff and they were pretty wound up. Then two big guys got hold of the dead guy's legs and dragged him out. They were gonna bring another one in. I didn't know what to do. I didn't think I could go through that again," Celeste said.

"But they never came back," Sam offered.

"Yeah. They were out there a long time and Ilford sent some guy out to see what the hold-up was. He came running back in a couple minutes later and said that the bums got away. One of Ilford's guys was lying on the ground and the other one was gone. So was the truck."

"I'll bet that made him mad," Nick said.

"He went crazy. He ran out and everybody got in their cars and sped off. I guess they never caught up with the bums. We were left there with the dogs and Eric loaded them back in their cages. After a couple hours, we just went back home. Later we heard the bums got away," she said. "I was glad."

"What about Eric now?" Maria said.

"I need to call him," Celeste said. "I hope he's all right."

• • •

Later that evening, Sam, Nick, Maria and Celeste discovered Eric's dead body lying next to the bodies of two of his Pit Bulls. He had been shot twice in the chest. The dogs had each been shot multiple times. Maria comforted Celeste in the car while Sam and Nick wiped their fingerprints off the door knobs and closed up the house.

"I'm so sorry," Maria whispered to the sobbing Celeste, as she hugged her in the back seat of the Landcruiser.

"They didn't have to do this. He didn't have the tape, I did. I should have stayed with him," Celeste cried.

"Then they would have killed you both," Maria said. "You got away. That was the right thing to do."

"We should never have done this," the girl sobbed. "It was so stupid."

Maria held the girl in the cocoon of the back seat. The sound of traffic mixed with the girl's sobs.

Chapter 29

Two days later Sam walked into the student union at the University of Pittsburgh and found Roxellana eating lunch. She saw him approaching and looked up.

"You again," she smiled. "You come to rough me up?"

"Mind if I sit down?" Sam said.

"Sure. Sit down. Hunky."

"Can't think of the last time I've been called that," Sam smiled.

"Change your mind about fucking me?" Roxellana said, chewing a large bite of sandwich.

"No. You change your mind about telling me what you know?"

"No."

"Doesn't seem like there's much hope for us, then," Sam said.

"There's not gonna be much hope for you if I tell Tommy you came back again," she said.

"Well, when he comes over to talk to me, I'll just show him this," Sam said, tossing the video tape on the table.

"What's that?"

"It's you fucking your professor."

"Where'd you get that?"

"It's the one you sent him. I got it from his office."

"So you are a cop?"

"No."

Roxellana grabbed the tape and put it in her handbag. Sam sat down and looked at her.

"Just a copy," he said. "Help yourself."

"Look Sweetie," she said. "You're a hunk. Why don't we get a room this afternoon. I'll pay."

"That's quite an offer and I'm flattered, but I told you, I don't have personal relationships with people I don't know."

"Bullshit."

"Maybe, but I think we need to get down to business here, Roxellana. I need some information and you have it."

"What makes you think that?" Roxellana pushed the sandwich away and got her compact out of her purse. She began to touch up her lipstick.

"Oh, wait a minute," she said, pulling her cell phone out of her purse. She opened the phone and fiddled with it, saying, it's set on vibrate and I thought it vibrated," still fiddling with the phone. "I guess not." She put the phone away and Sam continued.

"I know Ilford's men killed the professor."

Roxellana looked at Sam intently. She felt fear edging into her consciousness, but she continued to put on a neutral face as best as she could. She took out a compact and ran a new line of lipstick on her lower lip as Sam talked. She felt her lips brush past each other and instantly realized that adjusting her lipstick betrayed a nervousness. She put the lipstick down and closed the compact.

"I don't know anything about that," she finally said.

"Odd," he said, "since you were there."

"I don't know where you are getting this bullshit," she said, with bravado.

"Well, your father didn't tell me. He's dead too," Sam said, studying the girl.

"You don't know anything," the girl hissed.

"Well, Sweetie, as you would say, I do know that you're involved in the scheme to shake Ilford down for a hundred grand," Sam said.

Roxellana stood up. "Get the hell away from me," she said.

"Sit down," Sam said, calmly, tilting back on his chair. "I'm not going to talk to Ilford, but I need you to talk to me."

She sat back down, holding her books, staring at him. "What do you want?"

"I just want the names of the people who killed Inverlok."

"Why?"

"That's what I'm hired to find out."

"I don't know their names. They work for Tommy."

"So you were there," Sam said.

"I thought you knew all that," she said angrily.

"I'm just looking for your confirmation," he said. "I don't care whether you were there or not. I just want to know who did it," Sam said.

"All right. The big guy who did it. His name is Tiny. Now you know as much as I know. Are you done?"

"No. Now I need to save your ass."

"What are you talking about?" she said, hugging her books.

"This boyfriend of yours is going to be in some big trouble shortly, and if you're hanging around him, you're likely to get hurt," Sam said.

"You're stupid," she hissed, "My boyfriend has an army and he'll protect me. You're the one who's gonna get hurt."

"Look, your boyfriend is an idiot. He killed the son of a very powerful man who can hire him killed in an instant, and besides that, he's dumb enough to think he can go around killing people with dogs and not have anybody notice," Sam said.

"The police work for him," Roxellana said, defiantly.

"Yeah, he's got a few local cops in his pocket, but he doesn't have 'em all, and he doesn't have any of the feds, and he's gonna go to jail if he doesn't get killed first. Besides that, if you're still hanging around when they arrest him, you'll go to jail too."

"I don't think so," she said, her defiance a little less vehement.

"You're not dumb, Roxellana, so let's be accurate about what you're saying. You know you'll go to jail with him if he gets arrested because you're actively involved in the dogfight thing; it's just that you don't think he'll get arrested because he's the most powerful, richest guy you ever met. Right?"

She was silent, staring at him.

"But that's just a limitation of your experience. There are lots of guys more powerful and richer than Ilford. In fact, he's small potatoes. And you're smart enough to listen to me. I have nothing to gain by getting you away from him. I don't get paid for that. I'm just trying to save your life," Sam said.

Roxellana stood up, continuing to stare at Sam. "Thanks," she said, "I'll tell Tommy you were looking out for me."

Sam watched her thread her way through the tables in the student union. Her half-eaten sandwich lay on the plate.

Roxellana went immediately to the parking lot and got in her pink Mustang convertible, the one her father had bought for her, and headed for the Strip District, where

Ilford's office was located. Her afternoon classes no longer a matter of importance.

• • •

"What's the matter, Honey?" Ilford said, as she walked hurriedly into his office, tears streaming down her face.

"Oh, Tommy," she said as she walked around his desk and threw her arms around his neck, her books strewn across the desk as she collapsed onto his lap in the swivel chair.

"What's the matter?" Ilford repeated, pushing her upright.

"Tommy, this guy, the one I told you about before, the one that was asking questions about that dead professor, he came back. He followed me at school and he sat down at my table in the cafeteria."

"I'll kill him," he blurted out.

"Tommy, he told me he knows about your guys killing that professor... "

"What? How the hell could he know that?"

"I don't know. He didn't say. But he also knows about the dogfights. He's the one who sent you that letter asking for money. And he told me to tell you that if you don't pay up, he'll see that your ass goes to jail."

Ilford now pushed her off his lap, and stared at her. "When did this happen?" he said.

"Just this afternoon. I came right over after he let me go."

"Let you go?"

"Yeah, I was in the student union having lunch and he came in and made me sit there while he talked."

"Who is this guy? Do you know him?"

"I don't know, but wait a minute," she said. She reached into her purse and got out her cell phone. "Here,

Look at this," handing Ilford the cell phone. "I took his picture when I pretended to answer a call. Here he is."

Ilford looked at the grainy picture. He turned to the intercom and said, "Get Skeeter in here."

Within minutes, Skeeter entered Ilford's office and Ilford handed him the cell phone.

"Do you know this guy?" Ilford growled.

"That's the guy that the girl ran to. The one that beat on my sore hand. The one with the big dog and the guy with the shotgun."

"Sonofabitch," Ilford said.

Chapter 30

Richard Scuilli, the District Attorney of Allegheny County and heir-apparent to the Petragamo crime family, swiveled in his leather desk chair, the phone at his ear, the afternoon sun shining warmly on the blues and reds of the Persian rug in the middle of his office. He was silent, listening.

Finally, he said, "Yeah Tommy, I got that photo you sent me from your cell phone. I think I know the person you're talking about. He goes by the name of John Donne, but he's also known as Sam Budda."

"How do you know this guy?" Ilford said. "And why don't I know him?"

"I don't think he's been around here for very long, so it's not too surprising that you don't know him. Besides, he keeps a low profile. I know him because he managed to steal four million dollars of my money."

"What? And he's sill alive?"

"Putting holes in Sam Budda isn't as simple as you might think."

"Apparently not. But if he had four million of my money, he'd have holes in him even if it wasn't simple," Ilford said.

"People always say things like that," Scuilli said. "But I can tell you this, you don't want to start escalating threats with him. He'll blow your fuckin' head off."

"Come on, John. He's one man working with a buddy," Ilford said.

"You got that right, Tom, but it doesn't make any difference," Scuilli said. "If you want my advice, you'll avoid trouble with this guy. Whatever he's done — write it off as the cost of doing business and move on. It's a lot cheaper. That's what I've done."

"I can't believe what I'm hearing," Ilford said.

"How'd you get involved with him?" Scuilli said.

"He's got a tape of me at a dogfight where someone got killed and he sent me a letter telling me that if I didn't give him a hundred grand, he'd send the tape to the papers."

"How do you know he sent the letter?"

"He told Roxellana he sent it," Ilford said.

"Who's Roxellana?" Scuilli said.

"She's my girl."

"How'd she come in contact with him?"

"He followed her and cornered her in a cafeteria."

"How'd he know to do that?"

"I don't know. Good question. Maybe he thought it was safer than talking to me. It ain't."

"You're just illustrating my point, Tom. He has this tape of you at a dogfight, but there is no reason to think he knows anything about your girlfriend. And yet he does. This is typical Sam Budda. He does his research and he knows more than you think he does. And then he fucks you with it."

"Look Richard. This don't scare me. I don't care how he knows who my girlfriend is."

"You should care, because that might give you a clue as to what else he knows."

"He's just a fuckin shakedown artist, is all," Ilford said.

"Wait a minute, Tommy. You said Budda has a tape of you at a dog fight?"

"Yeah."

"That guy that got killed. Inverlok. The one you had me step on the investigation. Wasn't he killed in one of your dog houses?"

"Yeah."

"Don't tell me that Budda's involved in that too?"

"Hell no. He don't know nothin about that. He's just shakin me down for money for the dogfight."

"So it's just a coincidence that Budda turns up with the tape of a dogfight and that has nothing to do with your guys killing this Inverlok."

"Richard. I told ya. The college professor's got nothin to do with the dog fights. He just happened to be in one 'a my houses, is all."

"All right. I just want to keep track of what Budda's involved in. I don't want any surprises."

"The only surprise is that I ain't payin' him, John. I'm findin' him, gettin' the tape from him, and killin' him."

"It's not gonna play out that way, Tom," Scuilli said. "Just pay him. Do what I tell you."

"I'm sorry, John, but you're nuts. I don't know what's wrong wit you, but I ain't payin'," Ilford said.

"He'll chew up your boys and cripple your operation, Tom. It's cheaper to pay him. I'm telling you, it's cheaper. Just like you pay off the cops to keep your numbers operations goin. You pay this guy too."

"Richard, tell me in words I can understand, why do I pay this guy?"

"Tommy, you and I, we been around tough guys all our lives and you think Budda is just another tough guy. That's where you're wrong. Tough guys come and go. They work for money. Budda's different. He don't work for money. If he decides to destroy you, he won't stop, no matter what, until you're dead or he's dead. Imagine yourself swimming in the ocean five miles from shore and Sam Budda as a two thousand pound shark who hasn't had breakfast. That's what you're up against, Tommy. Listen to me."

"If this guy don't work for money, how come he's shakin me down for a hundred grand?"

"That's the part of the story that doesn't make any sense. That's not something he would do."

"Well, he's doin it."

"You'd better look into this before you do something that gets you killed."

"He ain't killin' me. I'm killin' him. I know I can't rely on these bozos I got workin for me to take care of Budda, but I got that covered. I ain't no dummy. My secret weapon's comin' in tonight."

"What's that?"

"He's Croatian. Fresh out of the French Foreign Legion."

"Jesus Christ, Tom. This isn't the desert. I won't say that I hope you know what you're doing, because I know you don't. Just don't get hurt too bad."

Chapter 31

Anatoly Grzyb walked in Ilford's waiting room, sized up the two men sitting by the inner door to Ilford's office, ignored them, and said to the secretary, "Grzyb to see Ilford."

"Could you pronounce your name again, sir?" she said.

"It's like you say Jib."

"Jib?"

"Yes, Jib."

Grzyb's head was shaved and he had an oversized forehead that stuck out like armor plate. The armor plate shaded tiny eyes that roamed whatever they looked at like cameras. His nose was flattened a bit, as if it had been beaten with a club. His mouth seemed to have a permanent downturn on the right side. The skin on his face was thick, like layers of canvas epoxied together, and lined from long exposure to the elements.

He was tall, a little over six feet, of ordinary build, but trim. He wore a black turtleneck sweater, black ankle length sneakers, and black field slacks made by Royal Robbins. The slight bulge under his short gray jacket was the stag handle of a ten-inch bowie knife that he carried inside his waistband.

The two men guarding the door assessed the threat, watching as Grzyb talked to the secretary. Who this guy was wasn't clear. They stood up and moved to either side of the door. Something made them uneasy.

For one thing, the bulge under his coat was a little disconcerting as was his shaved head and beady eyes. On the other hand, many of their visitors had cauliflower ears or flattened noses and scars running across their faces. Virtually all of them carried guns.

The secretary buzzed Ilford and said that Mr. Grzyb was here. She listened for a minute, hung up the phone, and said, Mr. Ilford will see you in a minute. Please have a seat.

Grzyb stepped away from the secretary and turned to face the door to Ilford's office, staring straight ahead at the panels on the door, five paces from the men who stood next to the door guarding it. His posture was straight. His hands were at his sides, the short jacket opened slightly in front. Ilford's men looked at each other.

One of them growled, "Hey, you. Sit down. Like she told you."

Grzyb just stood there, facing them and the door they protected.

The big men looked at each other again.

"I tole you, sit the fuck down," one of the big men said.

Both of Ilford's men outweighed Grzyb by a hundred pounds each, but they didn't move on him right away. Alarm bells were ringing in their heads.

Finally, one of the big men named Bo stepped toward Grzyb and extended both beefy arms to push Grzyb back. Before Bo saw Grzyb move, Grzyb grabbed his right wrist, pushed it into the other wrist and hit him in the solar plexus with a moving right cross. Bo crumpled and Grzyb instantly grabbed him by the neck and spun him around so that he was between Grzyb and the other man. Grzyb's right forearm slid across Bo's neck and the splayed fingers of his left hand rested in Bo's eyes, applying slight pressure. "Stand back or I pop eyes."

"Jesus Christ, Vinni," Bo gasped, choking from the pressure on his neck, "Jesus Christ, don't piss him off. Stand back." Grzyb's right forearm tightened on the victim's throat and he pulled the victim back tighter into his chest to throw his balance off. His fingers dug into the edges of Bo's eyes.

The other man, Vinnie, just stood there, his hands balling themselves into fists, his feet shuffling without moving, his mouth moving without talking. "You come, I pop eyes and I kill you," Grzyb said, evenly. The other man was frozen in front of the door, his gaze darting from Grzyb to his comrade, not knowing what to do.

The door opened from the inside. A large man stood holding the door knob. Grzyb pushed Bo to the floor, shouldered Vinnie aside, walked past the man holding the door, then stood in front of Ilford's desk.

"Come in. Sit down," Ilford said uneasily, standing behind his desk, his voice tense. Bo still lay on the floor outside the office, choking and holding his neck. He was directly in Ilford's line of sight.

"Not much skill," Grzyb said.

Ilford paused. "That's why you're here," he said, finally, gesturing to the chair.

Grzyb sat in the chair that Ilford was pointing to. It was two feet in front of the desk. "Close the door, Tim," Ilford said. Grzyb sat, his expression betraying no emotion. He sat easily, his arms resting on the arms of the leather chair, his eyes taking in the room. Two big men flanked Ilford and one stood behind Grzyb at the door.

"So you were in the French Foreign Legion," Ilford said, trying to ease into a conversation.

"Yes," Grzyb said.

"Your name is G-r-z-y-b. How do you say that?"

"You say 'jib,'" the man said, looking steadily at Ilford.

"Is that what you want me to call you, Jib?"

"Jib."

"What did you do in the French Foreign Legion?"

"I kill people."

"Who did you kill?"

"Who they told me. Who threaten me. Who get in my way."

Ilford studied the man, and then said, "I can't imagine anyone threatening you." Grzyb's oversized forehead made him look like some sort of armadillo. Punching him in the head would have been an act of futility.

"Then you know nothing French Foreign Legion. Legion full of killers. They threaten."

"How did murderers get into the French Foreign Legion?"

"Legion likes killers. Legion likes killing."

"Why did you stay?"

"I like killing too. And I have nothing else."

"Do you now?"

"I new with this. Out only months."

"Do you want to work for me?"

"What you need for me to work? You have men," gesturing to the two heavies standing behind Ilford.

"Yeah. I got men, but I need more than that."

"What?"

"I need someone who can eliminate a problem I am having."

"What trouble?"

"There's a guy who's shaking me down for money."

"That easy."

"Well, he's also got a film I need back and he's protecting a girl I want killed."

"No problem."

"This guy is supposed to be tough."

"They all say tough."

"You don't believe him?"

"Maybe is tough. No difference. I kill tough. But why not use these?"

"They tried."

"What they do?"

"Well, he stopped three of them by beating on my man's sore arm. He told them to beat it and they did."

"That it?"

"Not exactly. He also had a big dog and a friend with a shotgun."

"How many your men?"

"Three."

"What you do them?"

"Never mind," Ilford said. "I want you to kill the tough guy and his partner and I want you to kill the girl they're protecting and get back the film they're using to get money out of me."

"How much?"

"A hundred thousand dollars."

"Hundred thousand American? I do it, but need weapons and sometimes need men. Do it my way."

"Okay. You meet with my man Skeeter now and he'll fill you in on the details about this guy and his partner. Jason, you take Grzyb to Skeeter."

"I don't know, boss. This guy... he ain't one of us... "

Grzyb turned his full attention to Jason. His eagle-beady eyes fastened on the man's chest and face. In his mind, he ripped Jason's face off and threw the bloody skin on the floor.

Jason felt it. He took a step backwards, suddenly fearful, terrified in fact, and bumped into the wall. "I, I, I, I... didn't mean nothin, Mr. Grzyb. I didn't mean nothin."

Chapter 32

That evening Derringer and Zorba sat on stools at the Cutfahrt Bar and narrated their story to Dan, the bartender. Dan was an old friend. The three had become acquainted years ago when Dan worked at the Buffalo Gerty's Bar and Grill in the Strip District. Dan had been at the Cutfahrt for more than a year now, and he saw Derringer and Zorba nearly every day. He was incensed that anyone had been abducted from his bar.

Outside the bar, three men sat in a black sedan and watched the door.

"Mr. Ilford, this is Ricky. They're in the bar now."

"Good. Get 'em and take 'em to the farm. No fuck ups this time," Ilford said. "Put 'em in the cage and make sure they stay there."

"Yes sir," Ricky said.

The three men got out of the car. Two big boys and the small guy, Ricky. They all wore jeans and windbreakers. Ricky had on cowboy boots, the other two had on leather sneakers. Ricky was six inches shorter than the bigger men, but he was the brains of the operation.

One of the big men weighed in at 280; the other at 315. Both were over six feet and wore size 52 and 54 jackets respectively. One of the big men had a face like a shoe box, long and rectangular, with a ball cap on top. His buddy, leading the way in front of him, had a head that looked like a medicine ball, one of the thirty-pounders, with ears that stuck out like wings. Both of the bruisers followed the little guy, Ricky, who had slicked back hair, brushed straight back, and a face that was too pretty for the scowl he wore on it going into the bar.

Inside the bar, the trio spread out, Ricky in front, box face to the left and medicine ball to the right. Dan stood behind the bar wiping a glass with a towel. Zorba and Derringer sat alone at the bar. They saw the men in the mirror.

"Hello gents," Dan said. "Come in and have a drink." Dan moved to the end of the bar where he kept the sawed off shotgun and the ball bat.

Derringer smiled his crooked smile and swiveled around on the chair, facing the bruisers. He was thrown off his stride by their coming so soon, but he collected himself and began to go into what he called "impossible mode." It was impossible for him to ever walk again, they told him, but he did it. Now it looked like it was impossible for him to ever walk out of this bar again, but he'd do that too. A calm came over him. His smile widened and took over his weathered, creased, abused face.

"Come on in boys," he motioned with his arm. "We'll buy you all a beer," John said.

"You guys are coming with us," the little guy said. "Get up and come along. Nobody gets hurt."

"Hell, we'll go to a party if you're payin," Derringer said, "but we gotta finish our drinks and we'll buy you a drink too. All 'a y'uns." The smile played crookedly on Derringer's face. He sat there grinning, teeth missing, worn-out pants, all kinds of dirt and grease under his finger nails, and his pony tail held in place with a bandanna.

"Shut up, No-Tooth, or I'll take the rest of them teeth out," medicine ball said, gritting his teeth.

John laughed at the tooth gritting and pointed his finger. "Look Zorba," he said, "he's hurtin' hisself."

Medicine Ball walked three steps toward John, which was the worst decision he'd made all day. At about two paces, his balls ran right into John's steel toed boot, which happened to be rocketing on a course up to the ceiling. As Medicine Ball went down, John came off the stool, and Box Face was moving in. In a fluid movement, John's feet hit the floor, he lifted the bar stool over his head and crashed it down on Box Face's skull. Box Face fell like an imploded stadium.

Ricky had already sprinted past Derringer to the bar, where he had Zorba's neck in a death grip. He assumed that Box Face would subdue Derringer, but his two larger companions were already on the floor. Ricky was so intent on grabbing Zorba's neck and shaking him like a limp towel that he didn't notice Dan coming up on his right with the Louisville slugger. When Dan hit him, his head crashed into Zorba, and they both tumbled to the floor.

Ricky and Zorba were all tangled up on the floor when Box Face began to stir underneath the bar stool. Dan came over the bar with his bat. Just as Box Face looked up, Dan swung the bat and knocked him over an imaginary fence.

"It's a swing and a hit," Derringer yelled to the crowd that wasn't there. "He's battin 'em out of the park as fast as they pitch 'em. Damn, it's baseball history. This is a game to tell the grandkids about."

Neither Box Face nor Medicine Ball showed signs of life. Ricky was unconscious.

Derringer started another preposterous baseball narration and Dan said, "Shut your mouth, John, and get the fuck out of here. I'll call the cops. Take this bat with you."

Ilford's next conversation was with the police. Three of his men were in the hospital. Apparently they had caused some sort of problem at a neighborhood bar.

• • •

Two days later, Sam and Nick prepared to meet with Derringer and Zorba. They sat in Neid's Hotel and Bar in Lawrenceville, sipping draft beers, and waiting for the other two to arrive.

"Why do you think they killed the boy?" Sam said, starting a second sandwich.

"I don't know. If that guy Skeeter was involved, he could have just gone crazy and killed him," Nick said. "Pass me some nuts, will you?"

Sam passed the nuts. "Doesn't seem very smart. Now they got a dead body and some dead dogs and maybe some kind of police investigation," Sam said.

"I didn't say it was smart," Nick said.

"Here's what I'm getting at. I think this tells us something about our opponent. He's willing to be openly brutal, more than logic would suggest. He kidnaps the derelicts, he kills them in front of witnesses, he proposes to kill more of them in front of more witnesses, he sends heavies after the girl and probably the same heavies kill the kid. I think the only thing this guy will understand is not just being hit, but being hit pretty hard."

"You forgot. He's still sending the heavies after Derringer and Zorba," Nick said.

"Yeah. That too," Sam said.

"What do you suggest?" Nick asked.

I don't think John and Zorba will live through the week if they start messing with this guy's drug income," Sam said.

"You're probably right," Nick said. "If it comes to it, we can put them up in the Bloomfield house until we can get them out of town."

"Well, if they insist on doing this, maybe that's what we'll have to do. We can become an orphanage for bums and young girls."

Derringer and Zorba walked into the bar, got a pitcher of beer, and joined Sam and Nick at their table.

"Whut up dogs?" Zorba said.

"Woof," Sam answered.

"Tonight's the night," Derringer said.

"You got a plan?" Nick said.

"Yep.

"You got a backup plan?" Nick persevered.

"Nope."

"You got multiple escape routes for each location you intend to hit?"

"Hell no. Nick. This is John and Zorba you're talking to. We'll be lucky to escape at all. I'm limpin like an accident victim and Zorba he just don't move fast."

"Maybe you ought to consider going about this in a less dangerous way," Nick said.

"These guys aren't above killing their own people. They sure as hell wont hesitate to kill you," Sam said.

"Well, Zorba and I, we figure we was as good as dead a few days ago, anyway, so we may as well do some damage on the way out," Derringer said.

"What is your plan?" Nick said.

"We're gonna take out a few of his dealers is all," John said.

"That's liable to stir things up pretty good," Nick said.

"Yeah. So what?" Zorba said.

"So Ilford will be looking to kill you," Sam said.

"Hell, he's already doin that," John said.

"Yeah, but he might be a little more dedicated to getting the job done after you waste one of his dealers," Nick said.

"Probably so," John said. "Just think how mad he'll be if we kill more than one."

"You got the number," Sam said. "If you get into a bind and can get to your phone, call us up."

"Thanks, fellas," Zorba said, toasting them with his beer glass. "We think Ilford's gonna be pretty hot about this. But you know what they say, if you can't take the heat..."

Chapter 33

Grzyb sat at the head of a long table made out of two inch planks under a fluorescent light in a warehouse in the Strip District. A dozen large men sat at the table listening to Skeeter. At the end of the table opposite Grzyb, there was a large a map of Pacific Avenue in Bloomfield showing where each of the four cars they were using would be parked. Sam's house was circled in red.

The men had been in this meeting for three hours and each of the "team leaders" was required to get up and recite his team's part in the attack on Sam's house. The men at the table were not accustomed to military precision, discipline, planning, or constraint and they bridled against Grzyb's treatment of this as a military exercise. Nonetheless, they sat and they listened. Among themselves they all wondered why they didn't just bust in like they always did and waste the guy. No big deal. What the fuck?

The men were to be deployed in two groups. One group of four would enter the house and secure the occupants. The other group of eight would surround the house, contain any escape attempts, and deal with any police response. A strip of spikes was to be placed across the driveway. More bullshit.

If anyone escaped, they were to be killed quickly with silenced MP5s and their bodies carried to one of the cars. If escapees could not be contained or the operation were interrupted, the house was to be burned. If all of the targets had to be killed instead of captured, the house was also to be burned. Any tapes found in the house would be destroyed. Timing, weapons, and contingency routes were rehearsed for another two hours. Police response, if there was any, was to be stifled decisively and quickly. Three team leaders had police band radios and all teams were in radio communication.

They moved in at 4:00 a.m. the next morning. It was the dead hour. Sleep was deep. The men, dressed in black jump suits, surrounded the house like shadows. Grzyb and Giovanni went in the back; Skeeter and Leon went in the front. The locks were garden variety deadbolts, and the electronic picks which Grzyb had procured, opened them in a few seconds. The first indication that the mission might be fruitless was that there were two huge deadbolts on the back door that were not thrown. The second was that the door was also fitted with a Medeco lock that had not been activated.

Grzyb and Giovanni swept through the kitchen, dining room, living room, and bedroom, and met up with Skeeter and Leon, who were waiting, as planned, by the front entrance. Leon stayed at the foot of the stairs to secure the first floor and the other three slowly climbed the stairs that led to a closed door. Again the lock pick was used, and the door to the second floor opened. The second floor, it turned out, was a separate unit. The three men swept the second floor also and found no one. They took the stairs to the next floor, picked the lock and searched the third floor unit, again finding no one.

Grzyb then called in six of the men from outside and assigned them in groups to search each of the three floors for tapes. Grzyb himself floated between the floors and stayed in communication with the two lookouts outside. Grzyb directed that every piece of stuffed furniture be cut open and the contents of every drawer and shelf be strewn in the middle of the floor. Furniture was overturned, looking for hiding places. Holes were punched in walls, heating registers were ripped up. When nothing was found on the three floors of the house, the basement was similarly attacked. No tapes were discovered.

The men left the house, one at a time two hours later. First light was just on the horizon. They disappeared into the mist of the morning without a sound. The house was a wreck, the doors ajar. When the last man left, there was the sound of glass crunching under a boot.

Nick, his face painted camouflage black, watched from the bushes across the street as the intruders left the house.

Two hours later, as Nick scrubbed the paint off his face and Sam sipped coffee nearby, Nick said, "It looks like we're up against something new. There was clearly a plan and a chain of command. Lookouts were posted; multiple vehicles were used; a spike strip was placed across the driveway; the plan went into phase B when they didn't find anybody inside; and there was radio contact the whole time."

"Doesn't sound like the bozos who showed up the other day," Sam sipped.

"No. Also, they were dressed in black uniforms and carried silenced weapons."

"Well-planned," Sam said.

"Yeah. They really did a job on the house," Nick said, rubbing his face. "I don't think anything they left is usable."

"Looking for the tape?" Sam queried.
"I assume. What else?" Nick said.
"Probably us," Sam said.

Chapter 34

It was about 8:00 p.m. There was a November full moon, but the sky was overcast and the moon appeared only occasionally in gaps between gray-black clouds that could have been moving across a desert.

The Cadillac was parked near the corner of Davison and Fisk in Lawrenceville. The pattern was that the customer pulled up ahead of the Cadillac, the customer got out and walked back to the Cadillac. Sometimes they got in the back seat; sometimes they did not. The guy driving the Cadillac was black. He wore a white shirt with sequins and a necklace that had a huge pendant shaped like a dollar sign. He also wore a beret made of green felt that hung down the left side of his face and obscured his ear. His passenger wore a baseball cap and slouched in his seat.

Derringer and Zorba pulled up behind the Cadillac.

"Hey John," Zorba said. "Are you sure about this. I mean, we ain't done nothing yet. We can just go have a beer."

Derringer looked at Zorba. "Let's see. Ain't you the guy I got out-the truck a while back when they was gonna serve you up to the big dogs? Ain't you the one?"

"I know, John, but this here's gonna be messy."

"Hell yes, it's messy, Zorba. Us getting our fuckin stomachs torn out is messy too. Now if you're not with me, just sit here."

"All right, I'm with you. But I'm sure as hell scared," Zorba said. "I don't like this."

"I don't like bein killed by some dog fighter either," Derringer said. "Get off your ass and let's buy some shit."

Derringer got out of the van and walked to the sidewalk side, where he opened the large sliding door. He poured some liquid into his two gallon bucket and then filled Zorba's quart sized jar. Derringer closed the door and the two approached the Cadillac from behind, Derringer with the bucket and Zorba with his quart jar, Derringer going to the driver's side, Zorba to the passenger's side.

As he came up to the driver's window, the drug dealer looked around at him and said, "Whuchew wunt?" There were two men in the front seat of the drugmobile.

"I wanna buy some shit," Derringer said.

"Whuchew mean, shit," the drug dealer said. The dealer wore dark glasses and smoked a cigarette. Both he and his passenger were black and wore bandannas tied around their heads."You know, shit. Like you put up your nose."

"You put shit up your nose?" the dealer snickered. "You a weird motherfucker."

"You gonna sell me some shit, or not?" Derringer said, irritated.

"Hey cracker, you askin me if I want to smell some shit?" the dealer snickered.

"You wanta'a smell shit, go to a toilet," the other druggie said, chuckling.

"You boys ain't big into customer service. Looks like I'm gonna have to enlighten you," Derringer said, tossing the contents of his bucket into the car, two gallons of high test gasoline washing all over the dashboard and the two men in the front seat. Simultaneously, Zorba threw his quart jar of high test through the closed passenger side window. The heavy jar crashed the glass in the window and doused the passenger with its contents.

Instantaneously, there was the whump of gasoline igniting. The driver's cigarette ignited the fumes. The entire inside of the car was engulfed in flames. The occupants exploded out of the car, their arms flailing, their whole bodies on fire. One man rolled in the street, leaving charred patches of skin and flesh on the pavement. The other ran down the street until he ran into a tree, and then just collapsed in a heap.

"Jesus, John, There for a minute I thought you were gonna get in a heated argument with those guys," Zorba said.

Back in the van, they proceeded to their next stop, four minutes away, the corner of Butler and 53rd Streets. The dealer's Lincoln was parked on 53rd Street, facing up. A customer's car was in front of him with several people in it. Derringer pulled the van up behind the drugmobile and the two men repeated their drill.

This dealer was a surly white kid, baseball cap on sideways, wife-beater shirt, cheap tattoos on both arms, and fuzzy beard on his twenty-two year old acne riddled face. He watched Derringer approach in the rear view mirror. Derringer could see him watching, and altered his gate to seem non-threatening, some kind of old-guy imitation of the pimp walk that kids affected, adding one of the Derringer crooked grins, to boot.

This one was going to be more difficult because this guy seemed to be more aware. When Derringer got to the side window, the dealer faced him and said, "'Sup?"

"'Sup," John returned, holding the bucket to the rear.

"Whut yew got back there?" the dealer said. "Whut you want?"

"Oh, hell, man, that' jest my bucket," John said.

The dealer snapped a look at the passenger side and saw Zorba and his Mason Jar.

"Fuck you, man," he cursed as he started the engine.

Just as the engine caught, John and Zorba threw their containers of gasoline into the car, again, soaking everything, but particularly the dealers arms and the dashboard and the whole front of the dealer's body.

Before Derringer could strike his matches, the dealer jammed the car into drive and floored it. The Lincoln lurched forward, but the right front fender crashed into the trunk of the customer's car, parked fifteen feet in front of it and the cars' bumpers locked together. Steam shot out of the Lincoln's radiator. Cursing, the dealer jammed the transmission into reverse, then low, then reverse, but his car would not move. Helplessly, he stood on the throttle, burning rubber, throwing glances over his shoulder to see where John was. The engine roared at redline and the tires screamed, smoking — forward, backward, forward, backward — and destroyed themselves against the asphault. The thick, sickening rubber-smoke threatened to engulf the car.

Derringer danced up to the wrecked Lincoln just as the dealer was opening the door, and threw in a whole pack of lighted matches. The dealer went up in a ball of fire, as did the inside of the Lincoln.

The four kids in the car the dealer had crashed into piled out of their car and ran in four different directions, some up the street, some between houses, some through the park on the other side of the street.

On the way over to the next location Zorba said, "I didn't think he'd get so fired up over that."

Derringer just looked at him.

At Center and Schenley Farms Terrace the drug dealer's car was facing down Center on the wrong side of the street and no other cars were close. Derringer got his bucket filled and Zorba his glass, and they approached the dealer's car, just as they had the others, but as they approached, the dealer rolled up his electric windows.

"Hit the car, Zorba," Derringer said.

Derringer threw the contents of the bucket, ninety-three octane, on the car and Zorba tossed the quart jar through the passenger window. The dealer started the car and the rear wheels kicked up gravel and squealed when they caught the pavement, heading downhill to the intersection of Bigelow and Center.

The car was twenty yards away when Derringer fired his flare gun. The flare hit the side of the car and the entire vehicle was instantly engulfed in orange flame. Within another twenty yards the car crashed into a tree, bounced off, and then continued on until it ran over a six foot embankment and landed on its nose on the sidewalk in front of Schenley High School. Derringer and Zorba walked back to their van. No one emerged from the drug dealer's car by the time they drove past the flaming wreck.

Derringer looked at Zorba and said, "Just don't say anything."

• • •

The newspapers were full of the fiery demise of several drug dealers, burned to death in their cars as they peddled drugs in Oakland and Lawrenceville. "Vigilantes Take Out Scum," the headlines broadcast.

According to the newspapers, four alleged drug sellers, parked in cars, were burned alive in separate incidents when unknown assailants posed as drug buyers and then poured gasoline into the cars and onto the bodies of the men inside. They then apparently ignited the gasoline and burned the drug dealers alive before they could escape or drive away. The only clue the police had was that an unopened box of chicken flavored dog biscuits was found at the scene of the crimes, near the wreckage of the cars.

In the afternoon mail following the attack on the drug dealers, Ilford received a box of dog biscuits by special delivery. He was livid. Skeeter and Grzyb sat in front of Ilford's desk. Skeeter was agitated. Grzyb was calm.

"What is it now? Everybody thinks they can fuck with me. What's happening?" Ilford fumed.

"I dunno, boss," Skeeter whispered.

Grzyb said nothing.

"I want you two to find out who did this and kill them. You unnerstand. Kill them."

"Okay boss," Skeeter said.

"And another thing," Ilford said, "I want that guy Budda and that girl found. We got pictures of both of them. Put pictures out on the street. Five grand to anybody who fingers them for us."

"Okay boss," Skeeter said.

"Could be fires and Budda same thing," Grzyb said.

"What?" Ilford said.

"Budda maybe do fires," Grzyb said.

"Never thought of it. That would make sense. I busted up his place. He busts up my business. You could be right. That makes it all the more important to find the sonofabitch," Ilford said. "I want his balls."

Twenty-four hours later three drug peddlers on the south side phoned with sightings of Celeste. She was in the Beehive Coffee House.

Chapter 35

Celeste was maxed out on the violence. Eric was dead. The dogs were dead. Ilford was killing people with the dogs. He wanted to kill more people. If Sam and Nick hadn't stopped them, Ilford's men would have killed her too. And all of this was still going on. Any of them could be killed at any moment.

Celeste wrote a short note to Maria. "I'll be back soon. Had to take care of something. Celeste."

While Sam, Nick and Maria were out, Celeste left the house and walked a few blocks to Liberty Avenue, where she boarded a bus going downtown. In town, she switched busses and rode to the south side, her old haunts. God, she hungered for the old days of drinking coffee in the Bee Hive, snorting a little coke, taking a little smack, smoking a little weed. She needed that.

She wandered Carson Street for a while, looking in store windows and feeling like she had just been released from prison. These were her people. Hippies, hangers on, drunks, no-name people who sat in bars and coffee houses and made small talk and told jokes. She felt at home as she walked in the front door of the Bee Hive.

Unknown to Celeste, three street people had already made phone calls to the number they were given.

• • •

Once Maria found the note Celeste had left, Sam, Nick and Maria split up and went looking for her. After three hours they had found nothing and she had not returned home. Either she had run away or Ilford had her. If Ilford had her, they needed to know as soon as possible. And there was only one way to find that out.

• • •

Sam sat in his car in a VIP parking lot near the Cathedral of Learning, the engine running. Snow flurries landed on the windscreen and then vanished. The sky was overcast. Good Irish day.

On the ground floor of the Cathedral of Learning, next to the parking lot, Roxellana was depositing books in her locker. She was wearing a short plaid skirt and a thigh-length tan suede coat. As she closed the locker, a strong force gripped her left arm and whisked her toward the revolving doors fifteen yards down the hall. The person grabbing her was forceful and large. One of Tommy's big men must be protecting her from some kind of danger. Something must have happened. They must be taking her to safety somewhere. He always looked out for her.

"Just keep walking, Dearie," the voice said.

Roxellana glanced up. It was a woman. She was almost six feet tall with arms like a very strong man. Her thick blonde hair was pulled back in a braided pony tail. The woman was dressed in some sort of fancy black overcoat with velvet at the collar. She wore a white shirt and black bow tie.

"What the hell?" Who are you?" she managed to get out before the large woman's right arm cuffed her on the side of the head, just enough to knock her brain against her skull and disorient her, almost taking her off her feet. But though her legs momentarily failed her, she moved anyway. She was being carried in a kind of open bear hug by this large woman.

They got through the door and turned left, then down a flight of stone stairs. Sam's Audi was idling twenty yards away. As they approached the car, Roxellana's feet partially dragging with the strong black coated arm holding her up, Sam reached over and partially opened the passenger side door.

"In you go, Dearie," the blonde woman said, pushing her inside.

The large woman pushed Roxellana's semi-limp form into the seat, reached across and belted her in, and raised her eyes to look at Sam.

"Thanks, Gabriella," he said.

"My pleasure, Sir," she answered.

"My best to Mr. I."

"I'll convey your best wishes, Sir," she said, bending out of the car and closing the vault-like door. Sam locked the doors with the central locking system and backed out of the lot.

Roxellana was still too dazed to say anything, but she was coming around. Her coat was disheveled from Gabriella's rough treatment, and her skirt rode high up her legs from being pushed into the seat.

"What the hell, John Donne?" she said, regaining her orientation. "If you wanted to fuck me, all you had to do was say so. You didn't need to send your dike in to beat me up."

"Just sit there and keep your mouth shut ," Sam said.

"Just couldn't stay away from me, huh?" she said, straightening her coat, which was wrinkled awkwardly under the seat belt.

Sam looked at her and she could see she had him. He was just like all the others.

"I think Gabriella scrambled your brains," he retorted.

"Look," she said, pulling up her skirt. "I know what you want."

"You don't know anything," Sam said.

"Stop here and we'll get in the back seat," she teased.

"I'm not stopping and we're not getting in the back seat," he responded. "Just keep your mind out of your pants for five minutes."

"Why should I? That's where your mind is," she said, lifting her bottom off the seat and reaching under her skirt to pull her black thong panties off. She hung them on the shifter knob and looked at him with a coy smile.

Sam turned into Schenley Park and drove up the winding road to the top of the park where downtown Pittsburgh was visible. He pulled into a parking space facing downtown and put the car into park.

"You're gonna fuck me here?" she teased. "What will the joggers think?"

"I'm not going to fuck you at all," Sam said. "I brought you up here to talk to you."

"Why didn't you just talk to me then, rather than going through the kidnapping routine. Tommy is going to be pretty mad. His men are waiting for me and when I don't show up, they'll come looking."

"Yeah, well, they haven't done so well at finding things so far," Sam said.

"I don't know. They found your girlfriend, Celeste. What do you see in her, anyway. I'm much more attractive," Roxellana whispered in her sexiest voice, toying with the hem of her skirt, which was already up to her crotch.

"How did they find her?" Sam said.

"I don't know. All Tommy said was they spotted her on the street. Tommy used some of those photos of Eric's. He put them out all over the street. He's got a photo of you too, hunky."

Sam kept his eyes on the road. The atmosphere was charged.

"Forget the photos," Sam said. "Where is she and what has he done to her?"

"She's in the warehouse in the strip. I saw her."

"Is she Okay?"

"Yeah."

"Why did you go to see her?"

"Why do you think? If she blabs, if she says I was involved, I'll have a problem. He won't believe her, but things won't be the same. He'll always wonder. So I told her not to blab and I would see if I could get her out of there."

"Can you?"

"I don't think so. Everything is locked up."

"Maybe I can help. Do you think she's safe for a while?"

"Yeah. I think so. Tommy said he's gonna feed her to the dogs next week. I wish he'd feed her to the dogs today. Then I wouldn't have to worry about her any more."

"Why next week?"

"That's when the dog fight is," she said, unfastening the belt and curling her legs under her and shifting in the seat to face Sam.

"Does he know she was involved in the plot?"

"Oh, yeah. Skeeter saw her drop the tape. He knows."

"Has he questioned her?"

"No. I think he just plans to kill her."

"Can you draw me a diagram of where she is in the warehouse?"

"I draw a lot better when I'm naked," Roxellana teased.

"You're almost naked now, so draw," Sam said, handing her a legal pad and a pen. She drew the outline of the warehouse, the outside doors, the corridors, and the room where Celeste was being kept.

"How many men guard her?"

"It's been two when I was there, but sometimes that Grzyb guy comes. Sometimes he's there by himself."

"Who is that?"

"Some guy you don't want to mess with. Tommy says he's a killer from the French Foreign Legion. Tommy hired him to find you and kill you."

"Hmmm," Sam said.

"Come on, John Donne. I'm ready for you now. Just slip it in here," she said widening her legs and looking at him.

"Calm down, girlfriend," Sam said. "Why does Tommy want to kill me?"

"Cause he thinks you got the tape and you're shaking him down."

"And you're not about to tell him otherwise?"

"Are you crazy?"

"Well, that doesn't leave me much choice then, does it?"

"What do you mean?"

"I'll have to kill him."

Roxellana laughed. "Oh, Johnny. You're so funny. Tommy will squash you like a little bug. Johnny. Fuck me while you can, cause when Tommy gets through killing you, you won't be able to."

"Look, Roxellana," Sam said. "Listen to me. I don't want you to get hurt and I don't want Celeste to get hurt."

"You been fucking her, haven't you?" she said.

"No. I haven't been fucking her. Just shut up and listen. Your boyfriend isn't leaving me any choices. I'm going to get Celeste out of there, and, hopefully, I'm going to get you out of there too. And no matter what happens, I'm going to kill your boyfriend."

"Ok, Johnny," she laughed. "Let's just pretend you can do it. Why would you want to kill Tommy? Are you that jealous?"

"Because if I don't, he's going to keep hiring people to find and kill me."

"Well, you're right about that. But you could always just run away. You got a fancy car. Just drive to Mexico. I don't think Tommy likes Mexico."

"Not a bad idea, except I don't run away. And even if I did, I'd have to spend the rest of my life wondering whether every stranger I met was there to kill me."

"Johnny, I don't know what to do with you," she giggled. "You do everything wrong. You won't fuck me even though you want to and you won't run away from Tommy even though he's going to kill you if you don't."

Sam reached across the distance between them and grabbed Roxellana's jaw in his left hand. "Now listen to me you dumb bitch. We're talking about people getting killed here. I'll tell you once more. I'm going to get Celeste out of that warehouse and then I'm going to kill your boyfriend. You may not think I can, but I will. And when this stuff starts happening, if you're standing in the way, you'll get killed too. I'm trying to keep that from happening."

He released his hold on her face and Roxellana looked at him. He could see for the first time that she wondered whether or not he might actually be telling her something she needed to know.

"All right, Johnny," she said, straightening in the seat and pulling her skirt down. She took her panties off the shift knob and put them in her pocket. "What do you want me to do?"

"I want you to stay away from Celeste. I don't want to catch you in a crossfire when I go in to get her."

"If you haven't been fucking her, why would you risk your life for her?" Roxellana said. There was a hint of petulance in her voice. Or maybe it was jealousy.

"It's my job."

"That's it?"

"Yeah. Besides, it's not much of a risk. I've done this before."

"I don't believe you," Roxellana said. "These guys that work for Tommy, they're big and tough. Bigger and tougher than you."

"Yeah, I know. But that won't make any difference."

"You sound like Grzyb. He says stuff like that."

"Not a good sign," Sam said.

"What if I tell Tommy you're coming?" she said.

"Don't do that," Sam said, evenly.

"Why? What will you do then?"

"This isn't a game, Roxellana. If you tell him, he'll move her and he'll put more men on the warehouse. Then more men will die and I may not be able to save her. You don't want that."

"Why not? She doesn't mean anything to me."

"Because if she dies, you die."

"You mean you'd kill me?" she snorted in disbelief.

Sam paused and let the pause sink in. "If you talk to Ilford and he kills my client, I'll kill you," Sam said, putting the big Audi into gear and heading down the winding road in the spitting snow. Roxellana was quiet now. She looked straight ahead, the expression on her face like she had just been slapped.

Chapter 36

Sam, Nick and Maria sat over coffee in the living room of the Bloomfield row house. Sam told them of his conversation with Roxellana and her confirmation of Celeste's kidnapping.

"So what now?" Maria said.

"I don't know. Any ideas," Sam said.

"How about negotiating with Ilford. Give him the tape. Ask for the girl back. Tell him we'll leave him alone if he'll get out of the man-killed-by-dog business," Nick suggested.

"I like that," Maria said. "Nobody else gets killed."

"What do we do, just ignore that he killed John's friend with the dogs and then killed his own dog handler?" Sam said.

"I know, that bothers me," Maria said.

"Not to mention that he would have killed us if he'd found us in our other house," Nick said. "Those guys weren't carrying silenced submachine guns for no reason."

"Yeah, he would have killed us. He would have killed Celeste too," Sam said. "Do you think we can negotiate with these guys?"

"Hell, we been negotiating with bad guys all our lives, Sam," Nick said.

"Yeah, but this guy's gonna be all full of himself. He's the big crime kingpin. Nobody pushes him around. That sort of crap," Sam said.

"You mean he's gonna be thinking with his dick," Nick said.

"Yeah. And you know how the dick is. I'm the best. Nobody can beat me. Go fuck yourself. I'll turn you into horsemeat," Sam said.

Maria smiled. "I didn't know you two were psychologists on top of everything else," she said.

"Well, Maria, it's male psychology, so it's nothing too difficult. Men are simple. When it comes to being challenged, almost all men think with their dicks. Even more than when they are dealing with women. So the trick is to not respond too fast and give them a chance to think with their sense of self-preservation. If that doesn't work, then, as a last resort, give them a chance to think with their intellect, but that's a long shot."

"Do you agree with that, Nick?" Maria said.

"Yep. It's embarassing. Men aren't too swift."

"All right" Sam said, "let's start out by sending him a copy of the tape. Of course, we'll tell him it's the only copy, but we'll hold a couple copies back. See what he says."

Sam sent a copy of the tape to Ilford by messenger that evening. The next day he called. Sam identified himself to the secretary and got put on hold. Finally Ilford picked up the phone.

"Yeah," the voice said.

"This is John Donne. I'm the guy who sent you the tape."

"You are, huh? You know you're a dead man."

"Let's skip the threats, Okay?" Sam said.

"Hell, yeah. Why not? I'll kill ya with or without the threats," Ilford growled.

"You got something I want and I got something you want," Sam said.

"What's that, smart guy?"

"You got Celeste and I got the rest of the tapes," am said.

"Yeah, I got her, all right. And I got plans for her too," Ilford threatened.

"I know your plans, Ilford."

"You don't know shit, John Donne, or Sam Budda, or whoever the hell you are."

"I see you been doing some homework," Sam said.

"Yeah, I talked to Richard Scuilli. He told me about you, you piece-a-shit."

"Scuilli and I have had our differences, but he probably told you I'll keep my word. And my word to you is that if you turn over the girl, I'll give you all the tapes. All of them."

"Yeah, maybe. But before I'll consider that, you'll have to tell me how you made that tape," Ilford said.

"I didn't," Sam said. "I know you think I was involved in this, but I wasn't. The girl ran to my house and I took her in because I knew her and I didn't know why your goons were chasing her. It turns out she and her boyfriend were trying to shake you down, but I had nothing to do with it."

"Yeah, you piece-a-shit. Sure. You did it sure as hell. I know that. I suppose you used these kids to get the tape." Ilford said.

"I'm telling you, I had nothing to do with it. I don't want your money. I just want to keep you from killing that girl."

"How do I know you'll give me all the tapes?" Ilford said.

"I guess you don't. But I'm giving you my word," Sam said.

"Sure. Your word."

"You interested or not?"

"What if I'm not?"

"Then I take you out with a long range rifle."

Ilford burst into a fit of laughing followed by a fit of coughing. "Tell me how you're gonna do this, Donne."

"Simplest thing in the world," Sam said. "You're always moving around. I know where you are. I wait for you and shoot you with a sniper rifle at three hundred yards. Then after I kill you, I'll gradually dismantle your organization, one shot at a time. I may not be able to save the girl, but I know for sure that I'll kill you and I'll kill everything you have built."

Ilford remained silent for a time and then said, "All right, John Donne. You got my attention. How do you want to arrange the switch, the tape for the girl?"

"You know that park at the corner of Washington Boulevard and Butler Street, the one near the old state police barracks?"

"Yeah, I know it."

"Have your man there on the trail at the old WPA stone bridge with the girl at three o'clock tomorrow afternoon. I'll be there with the tapes. Just send one man with the girl."

"All right."

"And Ilford..."

"Yeah."

"Don't be stupid. No one has to get killed. No one has to go to jail. Just hold up your end and I'll hold up mine."

"All right, tough guy."

• • •

The meeting was set up for a wooded area within a city park where almost no one went. The park was a long grassy corridor bordered by a four lane road on one side and by a steep wooded bluff on the other. In between the bluff and the road was a line of grass next to a narrow woods with a trail running through the woods. There was a parking lot at one end right off the main road. From the parking lot, the meeting place was fifty yards down the trail and into the woods.

Sam was twenty five meters from the meeting spot nine hours early. The meeting was for three p.m. He arrived at six a.m. Rain dripped off the brim of his boonie hat. He lay on his belly deep inside a huge thorn thicket. He was wearing a Gore-Tex field jacket and pants with fleece underneath, but the cold radiated upward. He had been there now for six hours, moving only to urinate in a bottle. Right now, he watched the thin rivulet of water run off the boonie hat four inches from his nose. He held a Glock Model 20, chambered in 10mm, in one hand as he rested on his elbows in the thicket. The Glock was loaded with the original Norma factory loads: the two hundred grain full metal jacket truncated cone driven at twelve hundred fifty feet per second. His face was painted with green and black stripes and his hands were covered with black fingerless gloves made out of leather, Gore-Tex and Kevlar. He moved his fingers periodically just to make sure he could feel them. Otherwise, he didn't move.

Sam had a natural talent for sniper work. He had performed many long-range shootings for various agencies of government, which often involved laying up in thick cover, under layers of vegetation, tangled in thorns, baking under the sun or shivering in rain for long periods of time. It was something he had done well over a period of years.

Nick was nearby, on a ridge three hundred meters to his right, also hidden in brush with a scoped rifle trained on the meeting spot, which was just in front of Sam's hiding place. Nick didn't have Sam's long experience as a sniper, but he could kill a man at five hundred meters without fail every time he pulled the trigger. He was using a Steyr SSG chambered in .308 Winchester set up on a bipod with a 3-9X Kahles scope.

Sam and Nick had headphones and small microphones which facilitated communication. Information was transmitted both by voice and by code, using pre-arranged clicks of the transmit button.

Sam was hidden deep inside a tangle of vines, brambles and leaves. A careful observer would have seen or heard nothing. There was no indication of Sam's presence. He, on the other hand, could see the area around him. Behind him was a clearing, through a tangle of bushes and trees, the size of two football fields, and on the other three sides of him were open woods.

The only sounds were of rain dripping on leaves, and, high above, of leaves at the top of tall trees rustling in gusts of wind. Some leaves drifted down with the rain, landing softly on the wet thickness of other leaves already fallen. It was a cold early-winter rain. Small channels of water ran down the hill forty yards to Sam's left. Leaves landed in the channels and caught on twigs, forming tiny obstacles which the water quickly flowed over and around. Leaves, branches, and the ground were soaked into a chill wetness.

It was now noon. Three hours to go until meeting time. Sam was hoping against hope that Ilford would send two men in a car and that one of them would bring Celeste into the woods, where Sam would exchange the tapes for the girl, and everyone would go home in one piece. But something told him that wasn't likely. Nonetheless, because the girl's life was at stake, he had to try it.

Sam's mind wandered. He thought back over the years about the many times he had been in situations like this. Sometimes, it was the cold and the wet. Other times, it was the heat and the insects, possibly the snakes. You survived by telling yourself that whatever was around you was normal, what you expected. It was okay. You were all right. None of this stuff bothered you. In fact, it was not really there, not really important.

The cold was fine, the wet was fine, the fact that people wanted to kill you — and would kill you at the first chance — was fine. None of this made any difference. At the first opportunity, you would take their lives before they could take yours. It wasn't personal. It was just that's what it took to stay alive and it's what you would do. There was no glory in it. It was just the drill.

It was a little less than two hours until the meeting time. All quiet. Only the dripping now. Then Sam caught a movement in his peripheral vision forty meters to the right at about two o'clock. A pile of leaves had shifted. The movement was almost imperceptible, perhaps an inch or two. Sam stared at the leaves where the movement was. What at first appeared to be a pile of leaves was actually a mound of leaves. It wasn't there three hours ago, but it was there now. Imperceptibly, even to Sam, who had been watching this ground for the last six hours, that mound of leaves had materialized out of nothing. How long had it been there?

Again, there was a slight movement. The leaves were concealing a person. Ilford had a sniper. But how long had he been here? Why was he not better concealed? Had he seen anything? Had Sam been careless? Had he moved?

Almost certainly not, or he would be dead. He was glad that he had selected a position so deep in the brambles. His eighteen inch buffer from the outer edge of the brambles made it almost impossible, even for a trained adversary, to see Sam's camouflaged face.

Grzyb had moved the last few yards into position very patiently and skillfully, but he had been crawling for almost four hundred yards to get to that position. Not knowing the terrain as Sam did, Grzyb had started his camouflaged crawl too far back from the meeting point, and it had taken him three hours to get into position. He had entered the woods at a point Nick could not see. Once he was in position, he would study every inch of cover, just as Sam did. For all of Grzyb's skill, though, he had only been in situations where there was a great distance between himself and the target. Close like this, slight movements were easier to spot.

Sam watched the pile of leaves intently for any further sign of movement. Nothing moved for three minutes, and then the top of the pile of leaves moved slightly. "He's too close. There are other bushes out toward the edge of the woods he could have used," Sam said to himself. Then Sam caught a glimpse of movement again. "Christ, this guy is looking to get killed."

For most people coming into this type of meeting, Grzyb's lay-up would have been successful. And most people is what Grzyb had dealt with in the past. But when a seasoned sniper was on the other side, Grzyb's efforts were suicidal.

Sam clicked the microphone and then transmitted the signal for sniper. Then the signal for extraction. Sure, he could kill him. But he didn't come there to kill. He came there to save Celeste. They'd have to do it another way.

Nick signaled back that he understood and that he would cover the extraction.

Sam moved backwards in the brambles imperceptibly, an inch at a time, watching intently for the telltale glint of the glass pointing directly at him. It never came. Within half an hour, he had backed up seven feet and had begun to angle left behind a large fallen tree. When he got behind the tree, he could make better time heading backwards, away from Grzyb, for behind the tree he would be completely shielded from Grzyb's view.

Within an hour Sam had retreated twenty-five meters away from the meeting place and was in the vegetation along the edge of the woods. At this point, he was free to belly-crawl another twenty-five meters to an outcropping of rock, which would shield him completely, and then he could walk out of the woods, continuing in the direction he had crawled away from the meeting place.

At the outcropping of rock, Sam whispered into his mike. "Do you see my position?"

"I got you," Nick said. "I still don't see the sniper, though."

"He's twenty-five meters in front of my hide, a little toward the road. Right out in the open."

"That's why I can't see him. There a huge thorn bramble between me and him. I didn't anticipate a sniper going into the open. I thought I had everything covered by watching the thorn bush."

"I didn't either. If we'd been fighting, he would have been an easy kill. I'm going to hike down along the edge of the woods away from him another half mile. I don't need any cover now so you can leave your position. I'll meet you by the fire department training grounds next to the old police barracks."

"It'll take me about fifteen minutes to get out of here and back to the car," Nick said.

"That'll be perfect. See you then," Sam said.

Chapter 37

"Do you still want to go after Ilford?" Nick said to Derringer.

"You bet your Aunt Ferry's pickled artichokes," Derringer said.

Sam looked amused. "Pickled artichokes?"

"Just an expression," Derringer drawled.

"All right," Sam said. "You know they've got Celeste. We tried to negotiate a trade, but Ilford wouldn't do it. So now we do it the other way."

"What's the other way?" Derringer said.

"We break her out of the warehouse," Nick said.

"Now we're talkin'," Derringer said.

"We got to get her out of there before next week because Ilford plans to kill her at the dog fight," Sam said.

"The hell you say," Derringer said.

"Yeah. That's Ilford's plan," Sam said.

"We need you to watch this warehouse for us and let us know how many men are guarding it, what their movements are, and stuff like that. That information will tell us the best time to break her out," Nick said.

"I'll do it on one condition," Derringer said.

"What's that?" Sam said.

"You let me go with you when you break her out."

"We can do that," Nick said.

• • •

Derringer watched Ilford's warehouse for the next three days, calling in movements of Ilford's men. The pattern that emerged was that two or three men were at the warehouse during the day, but only two at night. Grzyb came and went at all hours of the day and night. They had not seen Celeste at all.

"Just callin in to let you know the night shift just.... ...hummmph."

"John, John," Nick said into the phone.

There was a crunching sound and then the phone went dead. Nick looked up from the dead phone.

Nick walked into the other room, where Sam was reading and said, "They got him, Sam. Ilford's got Derringer."

"All right, I was afraid this might happen," Sam said, putting down his book. "We don't have much time. Let's get dressed."

They had planned to go in for Celeste in two days, but the contingency plan was that if Celeste was being moved or hurt or if their surveillance was compromised, they would move immediately. They already had a rough idea of the layout and they needed to get there before Derringer got hurt too badly or the captives were moved. If they were lucky, Ilford wouldn't kill him right away.

• • •

Sam helped Maria into her bulletproof vest as Nick checked the weapons one last time. Sam and Nick would enter through a side door, using Nick's lock pick, or if need be, C4 explosive, as Maria entered the front. The operation was to be quick and silent. Maria, was armed with two handguns and an electronic device; Nick was armed with two .45's and an M4 rifle; Sam with a short MP5, which he wore slung on his back, and a combat knife. He was traveling light because he anticipated having to cut the captives free and carry at least one of them out.

The three left the Bloomfield house in three cars, which would be parked at separate locations. If one of the cars were blocked or disabled, the others would still be available.

At dusk, Maria, dressed in a brown UPS uniform, drove a UPS truck to the front of the building in the Strip District. Earlier, Nick had procured the truck to use in this operation. Maria exited the truck carrying a small box and rang the bell at the front door. Receiving no response, she banged on the door.

"Who is it?" a voice yelled from inside.

"UPS"

"Go to the side door."

"Already been there. No answer. Need a signature. It says urgent to a Mr. Ilford."

The door opened a crack and a huge man peered out.

"Gimmie the box," he said.

"I can't get it through that crack. Anyway, you got to sign for it," Maria said.

As he opened the door, Maria shot him with a 50,000 volt Tasar which she held out of sight under the box. Initially, the man just stood there looking at the projectile sticking in his chest, and then he started to vibrate as if he had grabbed a 220 volt line. Within five seconds, he fell to the floor. Maria pushed the door open wide enough to slip inside, stepping over his body. She then closed the door and knelt to make sure he was incapacitated. His eyes were open, but he seemed unable to move. She kicked the Smith and Wesson 9mm out of his hand, pocketed the weapon, bound his hands and feet with wire ties, and taped his mouth with duct tape. When he was secure, she headed down a dimly lit hall in the direction of the room where Celeste was supposed to be held.

Meanwhile, Nick's lock pick had opened both deadbolts on the side door and Sam and Nick slipped into the building, silently closing the door behind them and heading for the corner of the building where Celeste had been held. Three minutes later, they met Maria, who had encountered no other guards, and the three headed toward the prison room.

Roxellana's diagram had been reasonably accurate. In the room she had seen Celeste, a light shone out the open door and moaning sounds came from within. Nick and Maria took up rear guard positions down the hall from the open door to prevent others from coming in once hostilities started, and Sam headed noiselessly for the patch of light from the open door.

Sam did a quick peek around the edge of the open door and saw Derringer tied to a chair fifteen yards from the door. Celeste was tied to another chair in the corner of the room. Her head hung down as if she were asleep, or possibly drugged. Grzyb was standing in front of Derringer with a length of rubber hose, his back to the door.

"Make easy on self," Grzyb said. "I learn from you. Where this man is."

Derringer just moaned. His face was covered in blood.

"Talk... You live," Grzyb spat out.

Derringer moaned. Sam eased his way in the door, imagining himself as a cobra, sliding, sliding, quietly, smoothly, softly, quickly, across the floor, until he got to a fifty gallon barrel seven yards from Grzyb's back. The idea was to get out of this without shooting if possible. Shooting would alert other guards who might be in the building.

Grzyb's interrogation seemed to be going nowhere, and when he bent over to pick up something on the floor, Sam came out from behind the barrel, moving fast and silently toward Grzyb. As Grzyb was bent over, he sensed that someone was behind him and just barely turned his head when Sam's rear foot jab smacked him full force in the ass.

Grzyb literally flew through the air for a distance of three feet, until he collided with the wall. His head went through the plaster into the next room and his body hung limp on the wall. Sam had hit him with the power of two hundred pounds moving at a run, the right leg extended just before impact with a twist to the hips that gives more torque to the kick.

Sam knelt to free Derringer. He extracted his knife and cut the rope and tape that bound him to the chair, then gently lifted him down to the floor, wiping his face as best he could with the sleeves of his shirt. Nothing seemed broken and both eyes were there.

He looked up toward Celeste, thinking he would release her next, but he caught a glimpse of movement in his peripheral vision. It was Grzyb. He was standing, covered head to toe with plaster, and apparently trying to clear his head. As soon as he saw Sam, he went into a crouch. In a blur of movement, Sam saw that he now held a ten inch Bowie knife in his right hand.

Bowie knives are large, dangerous weapons, fitted with nine to twelve inch blades sharpened on the leading edge, but also on the clip, which may extend back from the tip four to eight inches along the top of the blade.

Sam moved without thinking. There was no time to unsling his MP5. His own Bowie knife was already in his hand from cutting Derringer's bonds. He pushed himself away from Derringer's limp body, shot his left leg out straight, and lifted himself to standing, but moving away from Grzyb. As he came up, Grzyb got a glimpse of Sam's Bagwell Bowie. The Bagwell knife, hand-forged by Bill Bagwell, is light and extremely maneuverable. Sam shuffled to the right, away from Derringer's body.

Grzyb's head, face and body were white with plaster and small chunks of drywall continued to fall from his head. He had wiped clear spots around his eyes and his mouth and he growled a low growl as he gripped the huge Bowie and circled in a crouch.

Sam had trained with Bill Bagwell, one of the two or three Bowie knife experts in the world. Bagwell is a knife maker, teacher, and master of the Bowie. According to Bagwell and others, the Bowie is the deadliest edged weapon ever devised. Unlike any other edged weapon, the Bowie knife can stab, cut, and back-cut with equal aplomb. This doesn't sound like much until you see it in action. Stabbing and slicing are fairly straightforward, but the back cut is more complex. Simply described, the back-cut is inflicted by a flick of the wrist backwards just as the forward cut passes out of the adversary's scope of vision, striking the opponent with the point and the sharp back edge of the blade, and potentially opening his face or his skull from one end to the other.

Bagwell, who has trained the U.S. Special Services, writes that if a modern Navy Seal or an operator in another of special service units were transported to a bar on the Mississippi River in the 1830's he would doubtless be killed within a few minutes by fatal strikes from a Bowie knife.

The knife Sam carried was the Hell's Bell model, favored by Bagwell himself, and featuring a guard shaped like an inverted horseshoe, designed to trap an opponent's blade as he thrust it towards you. The blade, razor sharp on the main cutting edge and on the top edge as well — called the clip — was eleven inches long. The grip or handle was six inches long and shaped like a coffin, narrow at the front, widening, and then narrowing again toward the back. It was made of mahogany and perfectly fitted Sam's hand.

Sam had been in knife fights before, but they were always quickly concluded, usually after his opponent sustained a cut somewhere, often on the wrist or upper arm, and became instantly convinced that this was not for him. But none of his opponents had been armed with a Bowie knife and none had moved as Grzyb did, like a fencer. Sam knew he was in trouble. Anyone who relished the thought of a knife fight was insane, and engaging in a knife fight with a man armed with a Bowie knife who appeared to know how to handle it, was a flirtation with premature death.

Fear edged into Sam's consciousness. He hadn't prepared himself mentally for this because he didn't anticipate encountering another Bowie. But he had been against knife fighters, and all one could do in any knife fight is remember the training. Move with control. Keep your legs out of reach. Strike and return. Use the back edge. Get him on the back-cut.

As the two men circled, Grzyb moved gracefully through the standard figure-eight angles-of-attack exercise in which the knife traverses the four figure eight patterns of angled attack – angled attack high, horizontal attack, vertical attack and angled attack low. Sam noticed that the figure eights were loose and wide, allowing Grzyb to use the weight of the weapon to carry it though the target area, a recognition on Grzyb's part that he was using a large, heavy blade that needed room to negotiate the corners. Sam also noticed that as Grzyb's blade moved, his other hand was in motion, moving in and out of a guard position and always ready for trapping or striking, grabbing or pushing. In short, Grzyb knew what the Bowie knife was about.

The two men circled each other, each wary. Grzyb was no less surprised to see Sam's knife than Sam was to see Grzyb's. He'd been up against Kukris in Indonesia and Pangas in Africa, but he'd never encountered another Bowie knife.

Both men held their left hand a little out from their bodies and the knife hand close in. Grzyb moved first. He threw a wide sweeping cut coming in from Sam's left which Sam caught in the hilt of his Bowie. Grzyb's blade was trapped and Sam twisted his knife sharply to the left, nearly ripping the weapon from Grzyb's hand. But somehow Grzyb managed to escape the trap and jump backwards, again in the guard position.

As soon as the block was made and Grzyb's momentum stopped, Sam stepped back quickly and withdrew to the guard position. Sam anticipated that Grzyb's next move would be a repeat of the first, this time with Grzyb waiting for Sam's block, and using the tangle of knives as an opportunity to strike with his off hand. Sam moved his guard to a slightly different position, and he could see Grzyb recalculating. He couldn't repeat the first move. Sam knew then that he was in control. He could anticipate Grzyb's technique, which was not complex, and he could block. The other man didn't know it, but he was at Sam's mercy.

Sam ran through some possibilities. If he lunged at Grzyb's right eye, one of his favorite moves, and then flicked his wrist to the left, moving the tip of the blade in a reverse propeller motion and catching Grzyb's skull as the blade started its downward arc, he could rip the center of Grzyb's brain out of his head by that simple downward propeller motion. If he performed a similar move on Grzyb's hand, the Bowie would sever all the bones and nerves of the hand, leaving the fingers flapping in air. But he was in control and he didn't need to kill him. He would strike shallow.

Grzyb lunged wide to Sam's right with a thrust, main edge down, ending in a thrust to the head, main edge up. Grzyb intended to flick the thrust into a back-cut to Sam's face. But as the lunge came, Sam stepped left and sliced the back of Grzyb's wrist in a back-cut motion of his own. Grzyb winced, but came back into the guard position, both men circling. The back of Grzyb's wrist was dripping blood.

Sam then initiated a shallow sweeping cut from right to left, and anticipating that Grzyb would come in behind the arc of his knife to cut his arm, Sam immediately initiated a back-cut before his forehand arc was complete and before he even saw any movement from his opponent. Sam's back-cut was in motion when Grzyb initiated his strike, and Grzyb saw it, but his brain could not process the information in time to withdraw and avoid Sam's back-cut. Sam's knife, whipping in the back-cut mode, sliced Grzyb's wrist again, this time to the inside. Grzyb cried out and danced to the rear, his knife hand now covered in blood. His teeth were clenched and he glared at Sam in a murderous hatred, the plaster flying from his hair as he shook his head in a fury.

Sam moved to Grzyb's left. Grzyb didn't seem to want to move in that direction, so that's the direction Sam moved. Grzyb was trying to pull his sleeve down to stem the bleeding, but it wasn't working. Blood was dripping on the floor. Sam made a feint. Grzyb moved, but not with the speed he had earlier displayed. He was worried about the cuts and he was slowing down. The bleeding was clearly getting to him.

Grzyb was now growling as he circled. His knife was making small circles and he bobbed and moved his left hand in ways meant to distract Sam. Sam stayed steady and kept circling. Suddenly, Grzyb delivered a powerful slash coming again into Sam's left. Again Sam intercepted the blow with the inverted horseshoe guard of his knife. The collision of blades this time made a clunking sound and this time Grzyb's blade was trapped. He could not withdraw it because of the twisting pressure Sam applied.

Sam twisted his own blade further to the left and wrenched Grzyb's blade free. Somewhere far off in the corner of his mind, he heard the big knife clatter on the tile floor. Instantly, seizing the advantage, Sam lunged forward, plunging the Hell's Bell into and through Grzyb's shoulder. The penetration was just below Grzyb's right collar bone. Immediately, Grzyb let out a deafening scream and fell to the rear, disengaging himself from Sam's knife and sprawling on the floor at Sam's feet. Sam's knife had gone entirely through his body before it was extracted when Grzyb fell. The top of Grzyb's shirt was soaked in blood and blood was quickly spreading to the floor. Sam sidestepped and kicked Grzyb's knife into a far corner. Grzyb lay there gasping for breath. His only weapon was gone and he was seriously injured. He looked at Sam with intense, but dispassionate hatred.

Nick appeared in the door holding an M4 rifle at the low-ready position. Sam was breathing hard, and was seemingly transfixed by the sight of his opponent on the floor in front of him.

"Are you all right, Sam?" Nick said, pointing the rifle at Grzyb.

"Yeah," Sam said. "Go get Celeste. I'll watch this guy." Sam stood over Grzyb, his big knife covered with Grzyb's blood.

Nick cut the ropes and tape binding Celeste to the chair and massaged her wrists and ankles so that she could stand. She mumbled something incoherent and sobbed as Nick freed her. Maria came in and helped lift Derringer into position so that Nick could get him into a fireman's carry while Maria helped Celeste. Sam walked over to Grzyb, who was glassy-eyed and breathing heavily.

Sam sheathed his knife, grabbed Grzyb by the shirt collar, and dragged him to a sitting position up against the wall. He extracted a large gauze compression bandage from his combat pack and ripped Grzyb's shirt open, placing the compression bandage on the wound, and wrapping a length of gauze around Grzyb's torso to keep pressure on the wounds front and rear. He said, "Keep pressing on the front."

At the door, Sam paused and said, "Your boss shouldn't have sent you out to kill me. Now it's gonna cost him. If I were you, I'd stay out of it."

When Grzyb, weak from shock and the loss of blood, looked up, Sam was gone.

Chapter 38

Nathan Inverlok and Sam Budda sat in comfortable chairs on the sixtieth floor of the U.S. Steel Building, which some people now call the USX Tower, in a huge room that commanded a view of all of downtown Pittsburgh. The room was furnished only with four overstuffed chairs, a massive Tabriz Persian carpet in the middle, and several mahogany sideboards along interior walls. Large black and white photos by Pittsburgh artist Norm Shum lined the walls. The effect of the sun coming into the sparkling light-sensitive windows on the deep purples and reds of the Tabriz was one of cheerful luxury.

Gabriella served coffee. Her hair was pulled back in a long braided pony tail and her muscles moved under the fabric of her clothes, a tuxedo-like dress that buttoned down the front and featured a vest and a white bow tie.

"Hello, Gabriella," Sam said, smiling.

"Good to see you again, Sir," she said.

Her massive arms rippled as she handed Sam his coffee with absolute steadiness. Her face was wonderful, Sam thought, with strong, almost masculine features, which nonetheless, kept pulling one back to the realization that this was a woman, and a beautiful one at that. She smiled at Sam as she handed him the coffee and said, "My pleasure, sir."

"That will be all, Gabriella," Inverlok said softly as Gabriella handed him his coffee.

"Very good, sir," she said, and left the room.

"On the phone, you said you had something for me," Inverlok said.

"Yes, I do. The good news is that I know the person responsible for killing your son. The bad news is that finding out who this guy is has me involved in some collateral matters that are going to have to be cleaned up."

"Who is it? Who killed my son?"

"The man's name is Tiny. He works for a small time, local criminal named Thomas Ilford."

"I see," Inverlok said. "Why did he kill my son?"

"So far as I can tell, it was an overreaction."

"What do you mean?"

"Your son was having an affair with a female student named Roxellana Jameson. The girl filmed them having sex and blackmailed him. She demanded ten thousand dollars or she would turn the tape over to his wife. He came to the place where Roxellana was staying, and that's where the trouble began."

"What trouble?"

"She was staying with a kid who handles Ilford's dogs, and when your son went there, she thought, to pay her, he started raising hell and demanding to know where the tape was. The kid who lived there got scared and called Ilford's goons. He told them someone was threatening Ilford's dogs. The goons came to protect the dogs, and in the struggle, this guy Tiny, a giant of a man, broke your son's back."

Inverlok stared into the distance and sat very still. "So Ilford himself wasn't there?" Inverlok said.

"No."

"What else?"

"Ilford keeps those dogs because he runs dogfights and makes money on the betting. After your son was killed, this girl, Roxellana, somehow got Ilford interested in her, and she is now Ilford's girlfriend. But she's greedy for money and she's apparently fond of the video tape thing. So she convinced Ilford to set up a dogfight where the dogs kill a man and people pay to watch."

"What?" Inverlok interjected. "You can't be serious."

"Unfortunately, I am. Ilford went for it because he saw it as a chance to make even bigger money on the betting. People would bet on how long it will take for the dogs to kill a person. Apparently, he's got some customers who will fly in from Las Vegas to see this thing.

"Of course, Ilford wanted the inside information on how long it takes a dog to kill a man, so he set up a practice fight where he was going to kill some derelicts and time how long it took them to die. Unknown to him, however, Roxellana had arranged for a hidden camera to film the whole thing, and then she sent a note to Ilford demanding money or she would release the tape showing him running the dogfight that killed someone."

"She's likely to get killed herself," Inverlok said, sipping his coffee.

"I've told her that," Sam said.

"You've talked to her?" Inverlok said.

"Yes, as part of the investigation of your son's murder. I needed her to confirm that your son was killed in the way another source told me he was."

"Who was the other source?"

"The former girlfriend of the kid who handled the dogs. The kid, Eric, told her about Roxellana's plan to shake your son down for money, about how your son got killed, and about Roxellana's getting Ilford to go for the dogfight idea."

"What about this Eric? Did he confirm the story too?"

"He's dead."

"What?"

"Ilford's goons again. They killed him while they were looking for this video tape. They suspected him and his girlfriend Celeste, and they were searching their house when Eric and Celeste came home."

"Why did they kill him?"

"I'm not sure what happened, but Celeste ran away from them taking the tape with her, and leading them to my house."

"Your house?"

"Yeah, my lady friend, Maria, had picked up this girl as a kind of homeless waif, she thought, and we gave her something to eat and some money. She said she wanted to get out of town. So when they started chasing her, she ran to our house. It isn't far from Eric's. And it's the only place she could think of."

"Did they catch her?"

"No. I was in the front getting into my car when she drove up. I held them off."

"How did you hold them off?

"Well, they didn't seem much interested in reason. But they got more compliant when they noticed Nick had a shotgun pointed at their foreheads and Ronin was looking at them in that special way he has."

Inverlok laughed. "Ronin," he said.

"It worked out pretty well except that when the girl was going inside, she dropped the tape, and they saw it. So they probably think that she works for me and I engineered the whole tape scam."

"Jesus. If they think that they'll kill you."

"That's one of the complications I mentioned earlier."

"This Roxellana, did she confirm the former girlfriend's story?"

"Yes, as to your son's death. She made no comment on her own involvement in the plot to shake Ilford down."

"How did the former girlfriend get involved in a scheme invented by this Roxellana?"

"Roxellana threatened Eric that if he didn't help her film the dogfights, she would tell Ilford Eric came to her with a proposal to shake Ilford down. Eric was scared and brought the former girlfriend in to help him with the camera. He couldn't start the camera and handle the dogs at the same time, so he got her to agree to start the camera with a remote switch he had rigged up."

"So they know this Celeste is involved in the plot to extort money," Inverlok said.

"Yeah. And it gets worse. Celeste got cabin fever holed up in my safe house, left the house and got captured by Ilford's goons. They were watching out for her. I knew that Roxellana would know where they were holding her, and with Gabriella's help, I pressured Roxellana to tell me."

"Oh, yes, Gabriella mentioned that she was going to assist you in something to do with the case on her day off," Inverlok said. "But she didn't say more than that."

"She was very helpful in getting Roxellana to talk to me. After I found out where Celeste was being held, I tried to negotiate her release with Ilford. He agreed to trade the girl for the tape, but he set up a sniper to kill me at the place we arranged to meet."

"I see," Ilford said. "How did you find that out?"

"I got there ahead of time and watched the sniper crawl into position."

"Okay. So that leaves this girl Celeste still in Ilford's hands."

"Well, yeah, it did. But when one of the guys I had watching the warehouse got captured, Nick and Maria and I went in and got them out."

Ilford poured more coffee, then settled back in his chair, thoughtful.

"So you have the girl back, but you aren't out of it," Inverlok said. "They still think you had something to do with the plot to extort money."

"Looks like it."

"They'll want to find you and kill you," Inverlok said.

"That's likely."

"And then there's the problem of this Ilford and the girl Roxellana. Neither of them killed my son directly, but they were both instrumental in his death," Inverlok mused.

"Yes."

"What do you think I should do to these people, Mr. Budda?"

"That's where our interests may or may not be in conflict. My associates and I have decided that when a thug likes this decides he's going to kill you, you have no choice but to kill him first. That may or may not be in line with your thinking."

"I'm in agreement so far," Inverlok said.

"Of course, if Ilford had no one to sell tickets to, he wouldn't be putting men in rings to be killed by dogs. Some of the men I'm working with now were among the intended victims of Ilford's first murderous dog fight."

"Yes. You have the suppliers of the entertainment and you have the consumers," Inverlok said.

"Right. And we have decided to deal with the consumers as well as the suppliers."

"Is that wise?" Inverlok mused.

"Maybe, maybe not. But it's our plan," Sam said.

Inverlok sipped his coffee and remained silent. Finally he spoke. "I assume you have thought this through. Feasibility, the likely consequences, probability of getting caught. Things like that. Probability of reprisals."

"Yes, sir. We've been over that."

"And you believe this operation is feasible."

"Yes, sir. We do."

Chapter 39

Cars of the infamous, the criminal, the sadistic, and the mindless arrived as much as three hours ahead of time at the Red Gate Farm on the day of the fight. Ilford's men patrolled the area in jeeps and drove among the early comers, most of whom sat on camp chairs around their cars in the field. They were tailgating. Mobsters, politicians and socialites mingled. Those who had brought grills shared their hot dogs and hamburgers and several others provided beer. The Las Vegas contingent, which arrived an hour early, kept to themselves around their limousines. The atmosphere was festive, jubilant. Death was in the wings. Excitement was in the faces.

Ilford's limousine was on the road heading to the dog fight when he got a call informing him that a large number of people were already there and some were cooking hot dogs over charcoal grills. Ilford instructed his guards to keep a close watch and to make sure no one was there who wasn't invited. Every car was to be checked against the list.

Roxellana sat cuddled up to Ilford in the back seat of the Lincoln Town Car as it sped toward the Red Gate Farm. She tugged on his arm and seemed to be trying to crawl inside his top coat.

"Tommy, I'm scared," she whined.

"Scared of what," he growled.

"I'm scared of that guy. I didn't think anybody could beat your guys. That French Foreign Legion guy is almost dead. Did you see his face. I've never seen a face so white. It looked like he didn't have any blood left. Skeeter said he may not make it."

"This John Donne got lucky," he said. "That's all."

Roxellana said, "I'm still scared, Honey. He said you'd go to jail. He said I'd go too. I don't think we should have this dogfight tonight."

"What the hell is wrong with you. You beat on me till I can't think straight to have this man-killer dogfight and now you don't want to do it. But I got thirty-five or forty mob guys from Vegas here to bet on the fight, and I don't have no choices. If I called this off, they'd feed me to the dogs."

"He'll kill us," Roxellana whimpered.

"Look, baby, I got armed men all around that barn and there are enough guns in the audience to outfit several police forces. You got nothing to worry about. I told you. I got it covered. Now relax."

"I can't, Tommy. I just know he's gonna be there and he's gonna kill us. I know it."

"Well, then, you know something I don't. If I had any more protection at the dog fight, there wouldn't be room for the customers."

• • •

It was an Amish barn, a hundred feet long and constructed of wide creosoted planks with a green roof. Entrance was up an earthen ramp and through a large double door, big enough for a tractor. There was a similar door on the other side of the barn, around back. The barn sat in a little valley, almost as if it were hiding, surrounded on all four sides by gentle slopes that rose up high off in the distance. The valley was three hundred yards across. On the slopes surrounding the barn fifty or sixty cars and trucks were parked. The owners were all inside by the time Sam and Nick arrived.

Sam and Nick pulled into the valley at dusk. Sam drove the Audi A8; Nick drove the Landcruiser. They came in together, bumping slowly across the field toward the semi-circle where the other cars were parked. Cadillac Escalades, Lincolns, several Mercedes S classes, a few Porsche's, some flashy Jaguars, several Infinity Q 45's and other high-end cars formed the semi-circle. Things had not really heated up in the barn by the time they arrived, but loud shouts and garbled noise was clearly audible. Now and then, a public address system crackled and someone said something that was followed by cheering and clapping.

John Derringer and Zorba had arrived an hour earlier and had checked in by radio. They were watching the barn from a tree line to the north using binoculars. Derringer's face was still bandaged and some of his ribs were still cracked from Grzyb's beating, which made it difficult for him to move, but both he and Zorba had insisted on coming along. As it got dark, they were to crawl closer to the outbuilding where the victims were being held and set up a shooting position. They reported that only one guard was assigned to this building. They were armed with handguns and a .30-06 deer rifle that Derringer owned. At the appropriate time, they were to use the rifle to shoot any guards they could see.

Although the crowd was shouting and cheering, the main event — the killing of the men — was reserved for last. The preliminary stuff, dogs fighting and killing each other, dogs killing puppies and cats, would be going on now.

Two men assigned to the parking area were visible as Sam and Nick drove in.

"Go left," Sam said into his communicator. "I'll go right. These guys are gonna check us out when we park. We'll split 'em up."

"Got it," Nick said. "Usual drill?"

"Yeah. Any other ideas?"

"No. They'll fall out of sight."

"Let's do it," Sam said.

Sam pulled his car up to an open space in a semi-circle of cars facing the barn. Nick was fifty yards to his left. Sam already had the window down when the man in the leather jacket walked up. He bent down to look at Sam and Sam shot him twice in the throat with a silenced Sig 225.

He powered the window back up and stepped out of the car, gun in hand, to check the man's vital signs. He was dead.

"All clear," Nick said, quietly.

"All clear here," Sam responded.

Nick was already in the clearing in front of the cars and the barn was almost a hundred yards distant. Sam walked toward Nick and they made a straight line for the barn.

Sam and Nick were both wearing their ear-protector communications gear and both had on three quarter length coats that looked a little like old western dusters. These garments were loose and covered a multitude of sins, such as ammunition harnesses hung across their midsections, combat knives taped upside down on the suspenders of the ammunition harnesses, two 45's each, one on the belt and the other in a shoulder holster, and one rifle each, slung under their right shoulders and hidden by the oversized coats. Both wore cowboy hats that covered their communications gear-ear-protectors. In the pockets of their overcoats were the silenced pistols, which they had just used in the parking area.

Sam pulled on Nick's sleeve as they walked toward the barn. Nick stopped. He looked at Sam quizzically.

"What?"

"One thing, Nick," Sam said, almost inaudible. "Spare the girl."

"The girl?"

"Roxellana."

"We're at risk here, Sam. We shoot until they're down. And there's a barnfull of them."

"I know. I know. It's just... just... if you have a choice."

"All right."

They continued walking toward the barn.

Sam and Nick walked up the earthen ramp to the door of the barn, which was flanked by two large men. They kept their heads down, talking in low tones as they approached. The guards were on alert. Two men arriving late wearing dusters and cowboy hats was enough to raise alarm bells. Probably just another set of tough guy wannabes dressed up in some stupid getup. Probably good friends of the boss.

When both of the big men stepped toward them, Nick took off his big hat and Sam raised his head with a big smile, then both came up with the silenced Sig 225's, which they had concealed in their hands behind the folds of the big coats, and fired point blank into the big men's heads. It was a drill Sam and Nick had practiced a thousand times. The only sound was the metallic clicking of the pistols' steel mechanisms working through the fire-eject-strip-chamber-fire cycle of autoloading pistols. The shouting and screaming from inside the barn was more than enough to cover that. Sam walked up to each man and silently shot each in the head again, then they both walked through the door.

Inside, a dogfight was going full tilt. Some of the men who had been assigned to guard the outside of the building were inside, standing in the various isles, watching the fights. That's how it always happened. Once the games began, security went to hell.

The crowd was on its feet and screaming. There were eighty to a hundred people circled around an area where the dogs fought. Some of the people sat on chairs; others stood; others sat and stood up higher on makeshift bleachers. Nick walked to the other door on the far side of the barn.

The crowd was an advertisement for diversity. Bloodthirstiness apparently knew no ethnic, sex, or age boundaries. The men were white, black and Spanish. Some wore plaid shirts or tee shirts and some wore two thousand dollar suits. There were big hats, like riverboat gamblers, caps, and baseball hats among the crowd. There were young and old, strong and weak. One man sitting in the front row had an oxygen tank. The guy next to him had a walker. A vendor sold drinks to the bellowing crowd, thirsty for death.

The wise guys all sat together, their strong Italianate features blending seamlessly with an arrogance born of too much money and too much power. Ilford and Roxellana were in the middle of the wise-guy contingent. Roxellana wore a striking pink outfit, low cut in front and back and, in all probability featuring also her signature short skirt. Ilford beamed beside her and turned enthusiastically to the men behind him, trading jokes and observations about the dogs and the slaughter that went on a few feet in front of them. A large man with a heavily lined face and thick gray hair leaned over Roxellana, his hand massaging her neck as he spoke in her ear.

The other women in the crowd were young and old, Spanish, white and black. Some of the younger women wore sparkly necklaces and gaudy bracelets. They had on party dresses and when they stood to shout, their faces contorted in rage or glee, their short skirts revealed shapely legs. One handsome black woman in a pants suit jumped excitedly as the dogs attacked each other. Her tits bounced and wobbled as she moved.

"Don't let him do that, you piece of shit."

"Kill that brown bastard."

"Bite the hell out of him, Brute."

"Tear him up, goddam it, King."

The dogs, Pit Bulls, raged at each other, lunging and circling, trying for advantage. Finally, the brown dog got hold of the white dog's font leg, but the white dog clamped down on the brown dog's back. The crowd went wild. The dogs growled and dug in their teeth. When the white dog actually tore a chunk of flesh from the brown dog's shoulder, the brown dog released his grip on the white dog's leg and let out a shriek of pain. The bones of his back and shoulder were visible where the skin had been ripped off.

Instantly, the white dog went for the brown dog's throat and clamped down hard, shutting off his opponent's air and quieting his shrieks of pain. The white dog was hurt — he couldn't put weight on his front leg — but he held on to the brown dog's throat and growled and shook his head. The crowd stood and cheered. Finally, it was over, and the body of the brown dog hung limp in the white dog's mouth. Cheering, clapping and whistling drowned out any sounds that the dogs themselves might be making. The crowd was on its feet and was ecstatic.

The referee stepped into the fighting circle with his wireless mike and set up an electronic screeching that competed with the sound of the crowd.

"The winnahhh, by a bite-out in the first round, is King, the Pit Bull from Philadelphia. Philadelphia King. Let's have a round of applause for this killah."

The audience roared and clapped and the owners of both dogs came into the ring. King's owner carried a hammer. All the time the announcer was talking and the audience was yelling, King was still biting and shaking his helpless opponent. King's owner walked over to him and hit him a solid blow on the head with the hammer. King whimpered and dropped to the floor. The owner kicked him with his foot to make sure he was too dopey to bite, then slipped a noose collar around his neck and dragged him out of the ring by his neck. A little cloud of dust rose as the dog's unconscious body bumped across the ring. The crowd cheered. The other dog's owner picked up the body of his dog, walked to the side of the ring, and threw it unceremoniously in a trashcan. The dog may have been alive or it may have been dead, but it made no difference to anyone, and certainly not the owner, because the dog lost his match and his fighting days were over. He would be disposed of with the rest of the garbage.

The announcer now had the ring to himself and said, "Ladies and Gentlemen, our next match is between two killer dogs from right here in Allegheny County, the amazing Rex, Dog of Death, and the astonishing Sampson, the Slayer. But for your entertainment, the dogs will not be fighting each other. They will be killing puppies. Each dog will have three puppies to kill and we will time them. The dog which kills all three faster will be the winner. Place your bets."

The owners of the dogs brought their dogs into the circle and walked them around on leashes, each growling, snarling and snapping at the other. Ring staff was on hands and knees swabbing up blood from the previous match.

"All right now, if the handlers will bring in the first puppies we will..."

He never finished his sentence because a forty grain bullet from Sam's FN PS90 rifle chambered in 5.7 x 28 mm, slammed into his forehead, traveling at about 2800 feet per second, and exploded through his brain, rendering it instant mush. A pink spray of blood and brains shot out the back of his head as he stood, his mouth open in what looked like surprise, just before his body fell to the dirt of the ring.

Within a second, Nick opened up from the other side of the barn with an AK 47, killing the puppy handlers and any security men who were standing in the aisles. He was firing controlled three-shot bursts. Puppies and dogs scampered wildly across the dead body of the announcer and into the crowd.

Outside, there were several booms from Derringer's .30-06. He killed three guards who were running toward the barn when the shooting started. Derringer and Zorba ran from the tree line and opened the cage for the five derelicts who were about to be sacrificed. They told them to run for the woods. Terror was in all their faces and they didn't need to be told twice.

Back inside, out of the corner of his eye, Sam saw some of the men in the wise-guy section stand and reach in their coats. He fired an aimed series of bursts in that direction.

The crowd itself was now largely on its feet and pandemonium was just starting to break out. It took five to seven seconds for the crowd to realize that people around them were being killed by gunfire. Sam and Nick were now completely engaged in firing into the crowd, their guns on full auto, sweeping in slow, gentle arcs across the raging bodies, all of whom were suddenly desperate to escape death.

The discipline was to shoot those who were closest first. The dead and wounded then formed a barrier that made it difficult for others to reach the shooters or the doors.

Nick's AK magazine held thirty rounds and it was exhausted first. He killed or wounded at least fifteen people before the reload. Sam had a fifty round magazine in the smaller caliber FN. When Sam heard Nick stop firing, he switched to semi-automatic aimed covering fire, shooting across the barn at people who were converging on Nick.

By the time Nick was reloaded, Sam's magazine was empty and he was reloading. This time, Nick covered Sam with the AK while Sam reloaded the FN. This was the part of the exercise that required the greatest control, the greatest presence of mind, the greatest dexterity. Magazines were being exhausted, people were converging, they were desperate and charging headlong, and when one shooter stopped firing to reload, the continuing shooter had to cover two targets at once, those charging at him and those charging at the man who was reloading. There was no room for fumbling. The empty magazine had to be released and the fresh magazine had to be pulled from the pouch and snapped into the rifle at exactly the right angle.

The charge was stalled now by the mass of bodies already fallen in the path of those still trying to escape. At this stage of things, short sweeping three shot bursts were the drill. The slower AK roared across the barn, boom,

boom, boom. Hot brass from the AK shot in a high trajectory as the gun belched its deadly hundred-twenty-five grain hollowpoints. Sam's FN fired so fast that it was hard to get any sweep at all into the aimed fire. The empties flew out the bottom of the gun with urgency, scalding hot, hitting Sam's legs as they cascaded out of the gun and piled up on the floor.

Sam and Nick shot men and women without distinction. Red stains appeared on white shirts; women sprawled across makeshift bleachers at bizarre angles, their dresses midway up their thighs, their hair hanging loose or spread across the body that lay under them. One man lay flat on his face five feet from Nick, his arms stretched out straight as if he were praying. A bodybuilder type had thrown a chair at Sam and lunged for him from the side. Sam swung the FN and shot him three times in the head. It was an undisciplined jerk of the trigger. When the bodybuilder hit the floor, he had no face.

By the time the shooters were on their third magazines, the twenty people who were still alive seemed to have gathered in the center of the barn, not knowing where to turn. They were in the dog fighting ring, clambering over bodies, running into each other and screaming. Sam and Nick methodically shot them all, firing from opposite sides of the barn, the AK banging its slower .30 caliber death rattle and the FN setting up a shriller, faster clatter of lethality.

The barrels of both guns were too hot to touch when the fourth magazines had been finished. Both shooters reloaded and surveyed the room. Here and there they saw movement and they could hear moans. Both Sam and Nick swung around when the doors on Nick's side of the barn opened. It was Derringer and Zorba. They were stunned by the scene before them. Dead bodies were everywhere and dogs were loose and running around the barn in terror or in cages barking and howling.

Sam provided cover while Nick began the check of the victims. He walked into the thick of the corpses and bleeding bodies, fallen on each other and sprawled in every available inch of ground, some facing up, some down. Some had looks of anguish on their faces, others surprise, others anger, others, abject fear.

Nick shifted bodies with his foot and shot whenever he saw movement. None of these bastards were going to walk out of here. Some of them may still be alive, but if they were, it wasn't for lack of trying to kill them.

Sam and Nick walked away from the ring and stopped at the door, looking at their work. Bodies and blood and the smell of death were everywhere. The only sound now was the yelping and howling of the dogs that hadn't yet run away.

"John," Sam yelled. "Get those dogs out of here."

Derringer and Zorba were already opening the doors of the last cages. Terrified Pit Bulls scampered out of the cages and made for the doors. No more dogs would be dying on this day.

As the last dog skittered through the door, Sam caught a movement out of the corner of his eye. Bodies moved slowly to the side and a head emerged. Both Sam and Nick had their rifles trained on the movement. It was the blood-splattered face of Roxellana. Her thick auburn hair was tangled into a hopeless brown mass that looked like a giant bird's nest; her pink jacket and skirt were stained with blood and she stood unsteadily, pushing the bodies aside as she did so. Sam and Nick lowered their rifles. She had somehow survived the massacre. She continued to push her way out of the bodies, struggling with the bulk of several large men who were lying against her. Finally, she was able to stand, weaving unsteadily and staring ahead, groping, in shock.

"Tommy," she whimpered.

Then, as if realizing where she was, she began frantically pushing and tugging the bodies, straining and groaning as she worked. Finally, she uncovered Ilford. His eyes were closed, but he was breathing.

"Help me. Help me," she screamed, looking frantically at Sam and Nick.

Nick told John and Zorba to leave. They headed out the back door.

Roxellana used her sleeve and wiped the blood from Ilford's face. It was impossible to tell if it was his blood or blood from the pile of bodies around him.

"Help me, you sonofabitch," she shouted over her shoulder, continuing to wipe Ilford's face. "What have you done? What have you done to him. Help me. He needs help," she bellowed.

Sam signaled to Nick, who set up a covering position.

"Goddam it John Donne, you can't just leave us here. Help me get him out of here. He needs a doctor," she screamed, the veins in her forehead straining. She was cradling Ilfor's head in her arms while shouting at Sam.

Sam waded into the bodies, moving carefully and slowly, the rifle tucked under his armpit, pointed toward Ilford and Roxellana. Roxellana kept up a constant invective, cursing him, demanding help, screaming for a doctor. Finally, Sam reached the spot where she cradled Ilford's head in her lap, bodies crowding her on every side, and stuck the muzzle in Ilford's face.

"Get that away from him, you bastard. You fucking killer. You sonofabitch," she screamed, slapping the muzzle away from Ilford's face, her countenance a mask of glaring, unadulterated hatred.

Sam shifted slightly and whipped the butt of the rifle up suddenly, striking her on the chin. The blow knocked her back, and she lay on the pile of bodies, unconscious.

Sam shifted the rifle to his left hand and drew the .45 from his belt. He shot Ilford once in the forehead. The two hundred thirty grain G.I. ball lodged in the far side of his skull.

Sam reholstered the weapon and backed out of the sea of bodies, struggling to keep his balance and watchful for threats that might unexpectedly emerge from the pile of bodies. When he and Nick reached the doors, Roxellana was still unconscious, sprawled on the corpses surrounding her. Outside, no hostiles remained alive.

Without speaking, Sam and Nick went to their separate cars and stowed their gear. Derringer and Zorba were already headed toward their car, which was about a mile away in the woods. The barn was eerily quiet. There was no other movement or sound except for the occasional howling of the dogs as they ran loose through the parked cars, kicking up little clouds of dust when they changed direction. They ran as if possessed, first through one aisle and then another, and then around in circles. Sam and Nick got in their vehicles and slowly drove to the main road. The other cars remained in place. When they got on the highway, Sam dialed his phone.

"Humane Officer Hanley speaking," a voice answered.

"There is a large barn in Bell Township near Route 819, five miles from the water reservoir. They've been having dog fights there. If you go there now, you will find a lot of dogs who need your help."

"Who is this?"

Sam pushed the disconnect button.

As he drove, he kept thinking of a line from The Battle of Maldon, "There was great slaughter on the field that day." The year was 961 AD and the place was the River Blackwater in Essex. Viking raiders slaughtered Anglo Saxon defenders. The soil was soaked with blood.